STONE ARCH BOOKS
a capstone imprint

Stone Arch Books™

Published in 2014
A Capstone Imprint
1710 Roe Crest Drive
North Mankato, MN 56003
www.capstonepub.com

Originally published by DC Comics in the U.S. in
single magazine form as The Batman Strikes! #5.
Copyright © 2014 DC Comics. All Rights Reserved.

DC Comics
1700 Broadway, New York, NY 10019
A Warner Bros. Entertainment Company

Printed in China.
032014 008085LEOF14

Cataloging-in-Publication Data is available at the
Library of Congress website:
ISBN: 978-1-4342-9210-0 (library binding)

Summary: Scarface and the Ventriloquist are
back. When they attach an explosive mini-Scarface
dummy to Batman's arm, can Batman escape
Scarface's trap without destroying Gotham City?

STONE ARCH BOOKS
Ashley C. Andersen Zantop *Publisher*
Michael Dahl *Editorial Director*
Sean Tulien *Editor*
Heather Kindseth *Creative Director*
Bob Lentz and Hilary Wacholz *Designers*
Tori Abraham *Production Specialist*

DC COMICS
Joan Hilty & Harvey Richards *Original U.S. Editors*
Jeff Matsuda & Dave McCaig *Cover Artists*

SCARFACE IS GONNA GO BOOM!

BILL MATHENY ....WRITER
CHRISTOPHER JONES ....PENCILLER
TERRY BEATTY ....INKER
HEROIC AGE...COLORIST
PAT BROSSEAU ....LETTERER

BATMAN CREATED BY BOB KANE

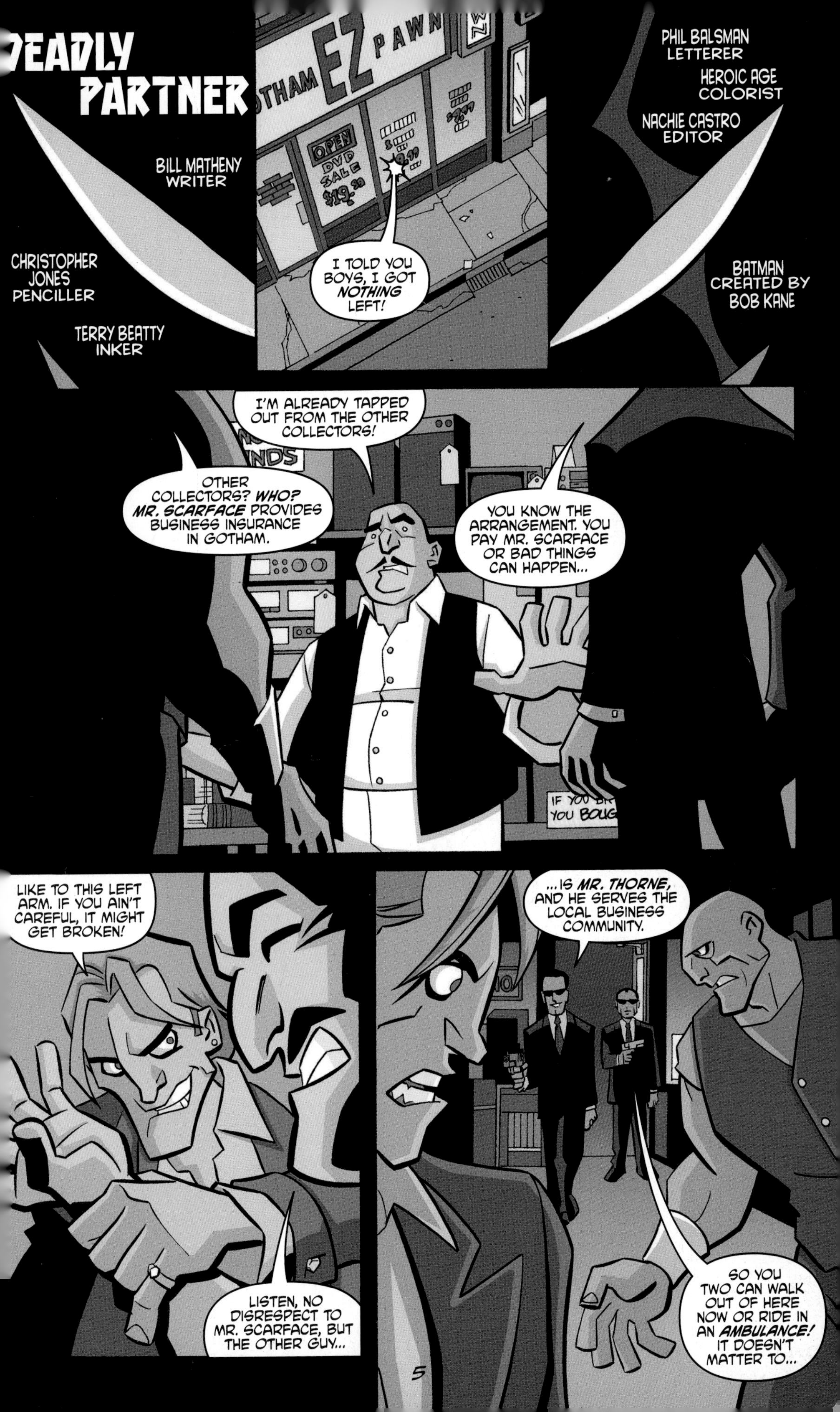

DEADLY PARTNER
BILL MATHENY WRITER
CHRISTOPHER JONES PENCILLER
TERRY BEATTY INKER
GOTHAM EZ PAWN
OPEN DVD SALE $19.99
I TOLD YOU BOYS, I GOT NOTHING LEFT!
PHIL BALSMAN LETTERER
HEROIC AGE COLORIST
NACHIE CASTRO EDITOR
BATMAN CREATED BY BOB KANE
I'M ALREADY TAPPED OUT FROM THE OTHER COLLECTORS!
OTHER COLLECTORS? WHO? MR. SCARFACE PROVIDES BUSINESS INSURANCE IN GOTHAM.
YOU KNOW THE ARRANGEMENT. YOU PAY MR. SCARFACE OR BAD THINGS CAN HAPPEN...
LIKE TO THIS LEFT ARM. IF YOU AIN'T CAREFUL, IT MIGHT GET BROKEN!
LISTEN, NO DISRESPECT TO MR. SCARFACE, BUT THE OTHER GUY...
...IS MR. THORNE, AND HE SERVES THE LOCAL BUSINESS COMMUNITY.
SO YOU TWO CAN WALK OUT OF HERE NOW OR RIDE IN AN AMBULANCE! IT DOESN'T MATTER TO...

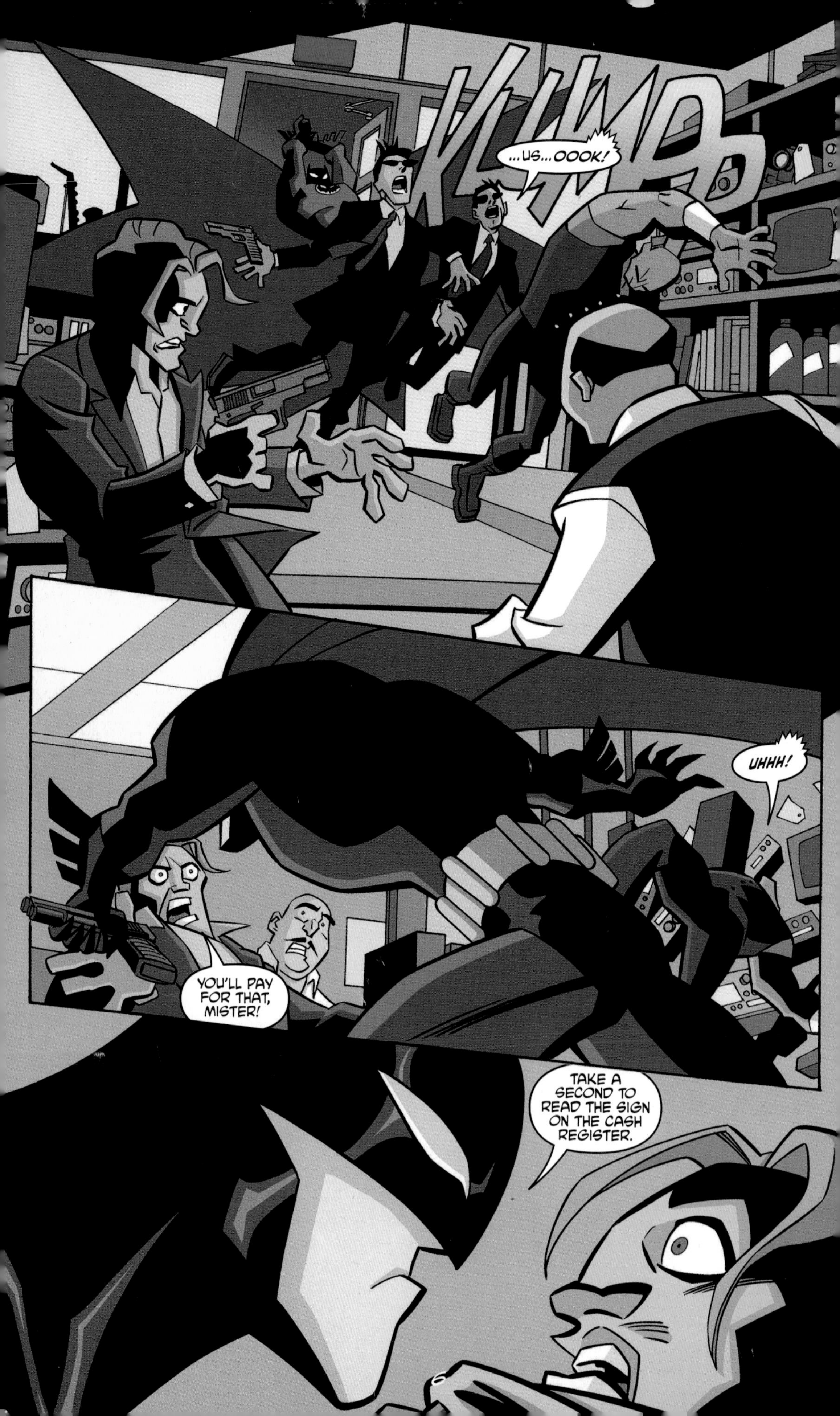
KLUMP
...US...OOOK!
UHHH!
YOU'LL PAY FOR THAT, MISTER!
TAKE A SECOND TO READ THE SIGN ON THE CASH REGISTER.

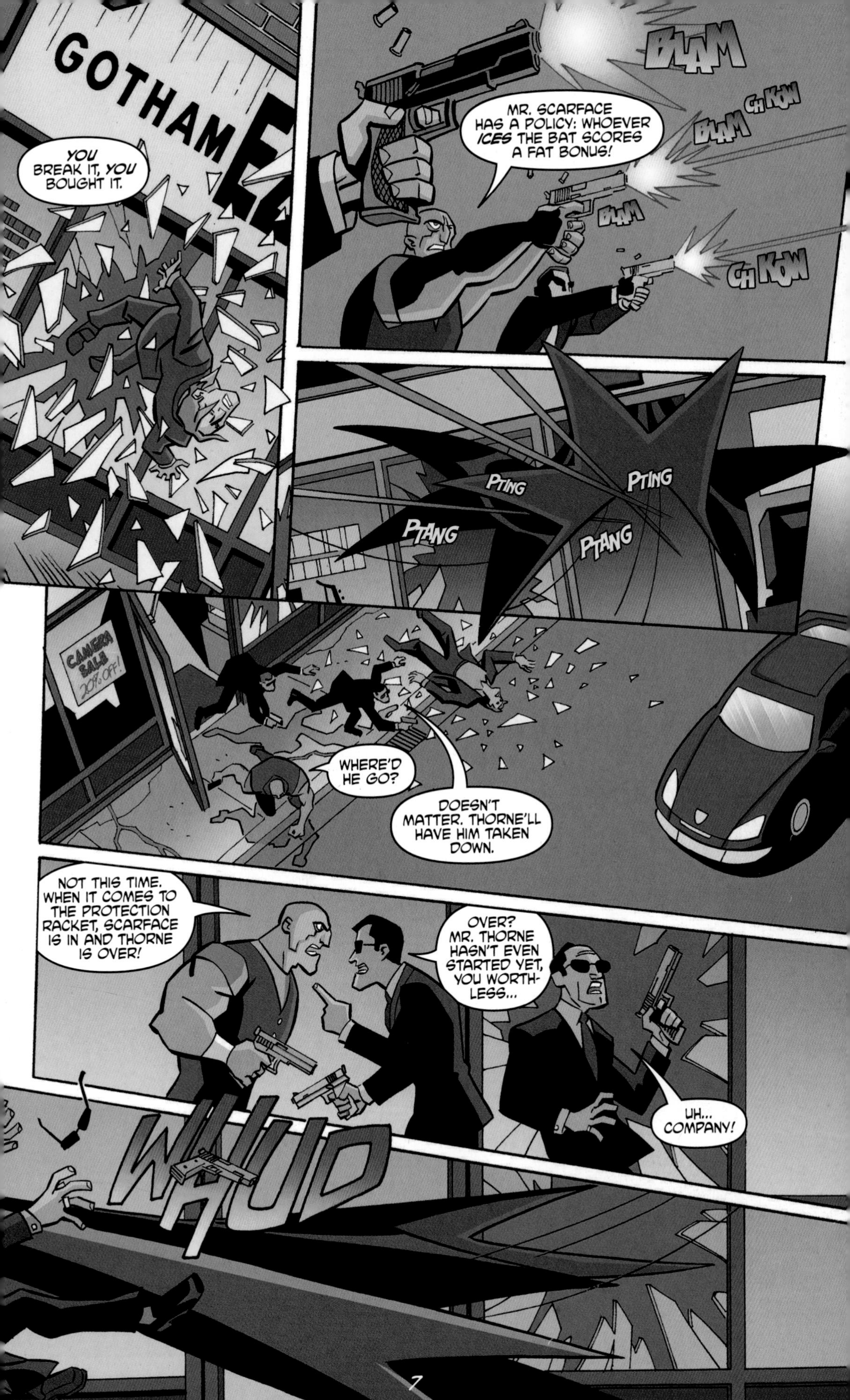
GOTHAM
YOU BREAK IT, YOU BOUGHT IT.
BLAM
MR. SCARFACE HAS A POLICY: WHOEVER ICES THE BAT SCORES A FAT BONUS!
BLAM CH KOW
BLAM
CH KOW
PTING
PTING
PTANG
PTANG
CAMERA SALE 20% OFF!
WHERE'D HE GO?
DOESN'T MATTER. THORNE'LL HAVE HIM TAKEN DOWN.
NOT THIS TIME. WHEN IT COMES TO THE PROTECTION RACKET, SCARFACE IS IN AND THORNE IS OVER!
OVER? MR. THORNE HASN'T EVEN STARTED YET, YOU WORTHLESS...
UH... COMPANY!
WHUD

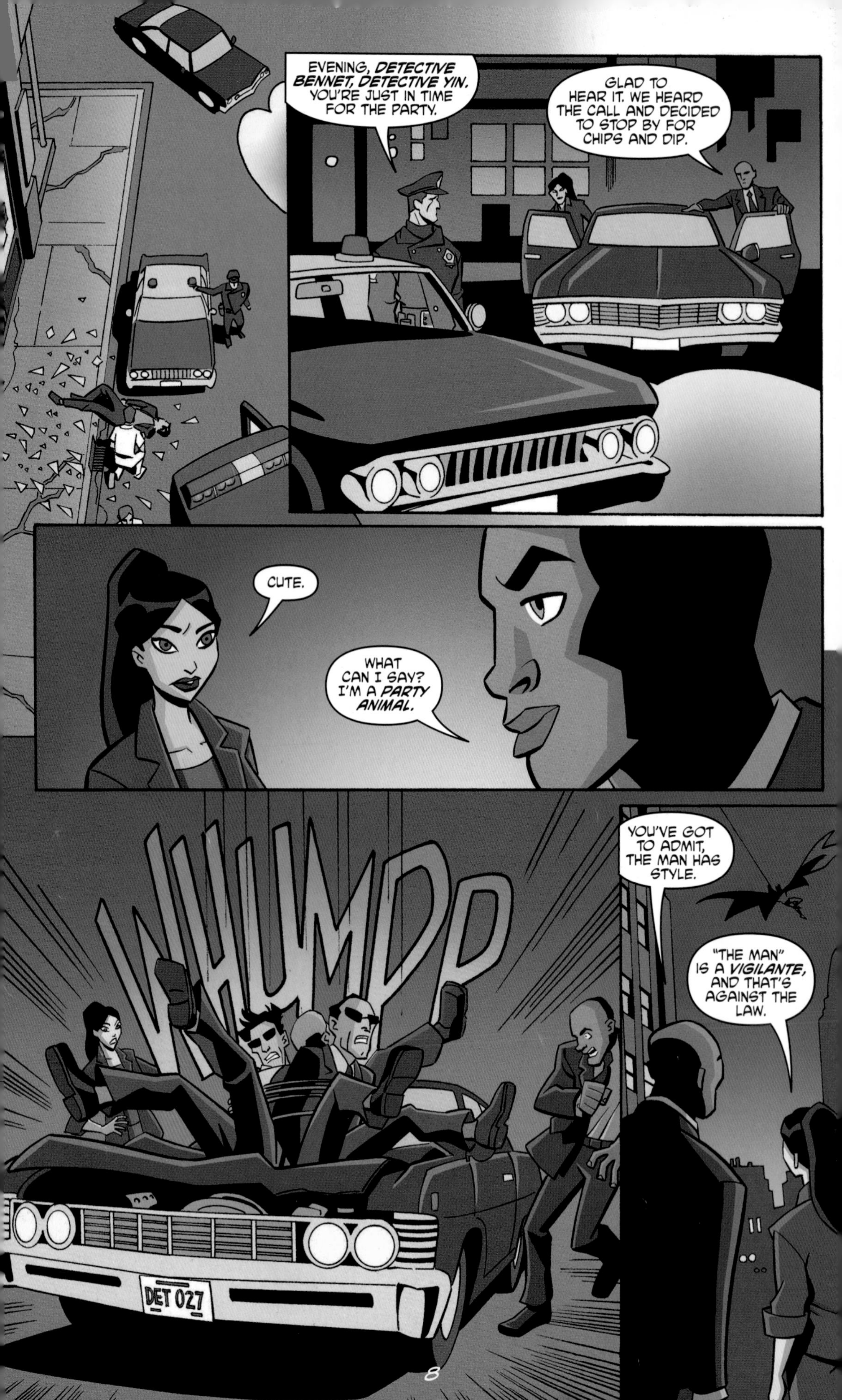

EVENING, *DETECTIVE BENNET, DETECTIVE YIN.* YOU'RE JUST IN TIME FOR THE PARTY.
GLAD TO HEAR IT. WE HEARD THE CALL AND DECIDED TO STOP BY FOR CHIPS AND DIP.
CUTE.
WHAT CAN I SAY? I'M A *PARTY ANIMAL.*
WHUMP
YOU'VE GOT TO ADMIT, THE MAN HAS STYLE.
"THE MAN" IS A *VIGILANTE,* AND THAT'S AGAINST THE LAW.
DET 027

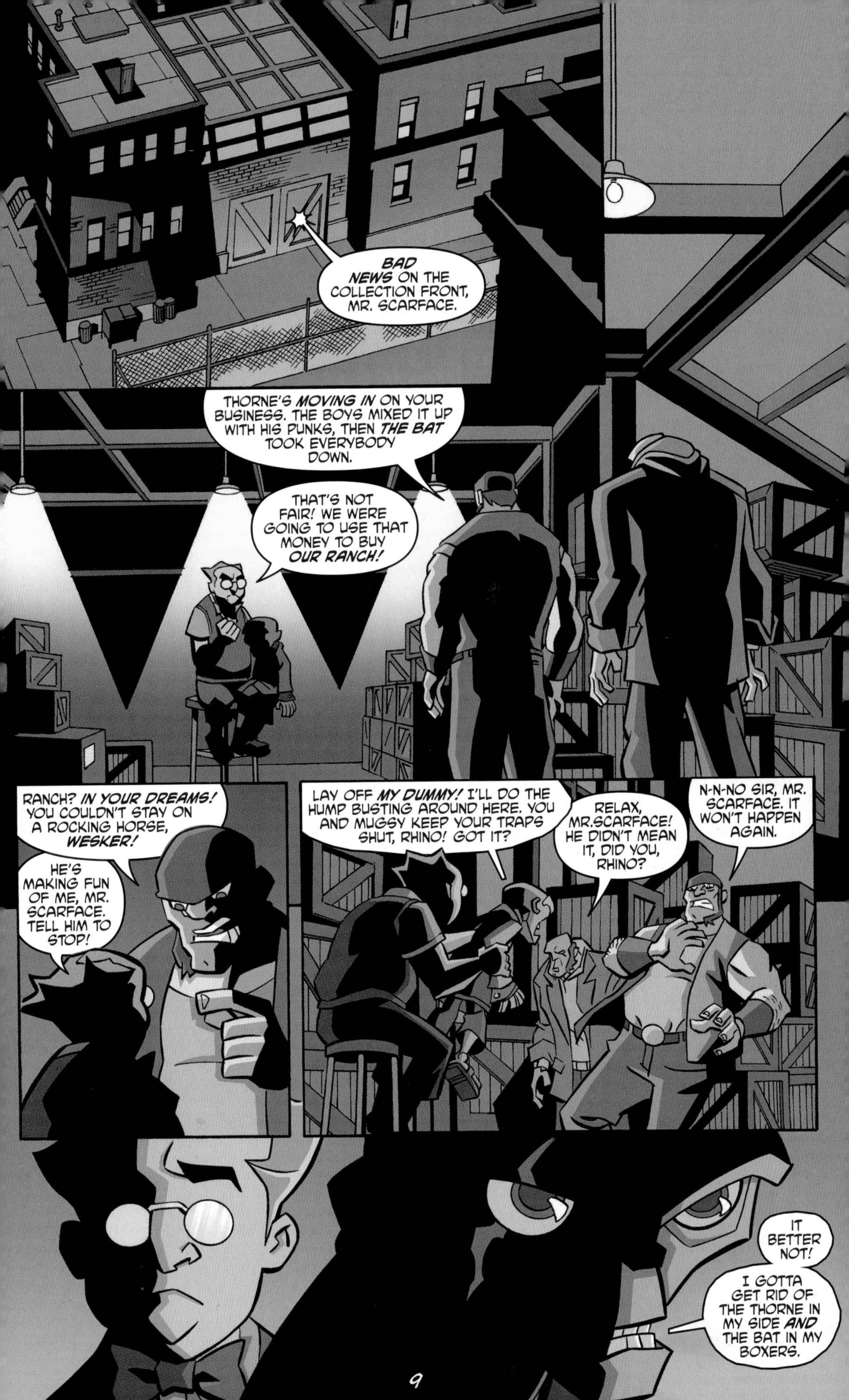
BAD NEWS ON THE COLLECTION FRONT, MR. SCARFACE.
THORNE'S MOVING IN ON YOUR BUSINESS. THE BOYS MIXED IT UP WITH HIS PUNKS, THEN THE BAT TOOK EVERYBODY DOWN.
THAT'S NOT FAIR! WE WERE GOING TO USE THAT MONEY TO BUY OUR RANCH!
RANCH? IN YOUR DREAMS! YOU COULDN'T STAY ON A ROCKING HORSE, WESKER!
HE'S MAKING FUN OF ME, MR. SCARFACE. TELL HIM TO STOP!
LAY OFF MY DUMMY! I'LL DO THE HUMP BUSTING AROUND HERE. YOU AND MUGSY KEEP YOUR TRAPS SHUT, RHINO! GOT IT?
RELAX, MR.SCARFACE! HE DIDN'T MEAN IT, DID YOU, RHINO?
N-N-NO SIR, MR. SCARFACE. IT WON'T HAPPEN AGAIN.
IT BETTER NOT!
I GOTTA GET RID OF THE THORNE IN MY SIDE AND THE BAT IN MY BOXERS.

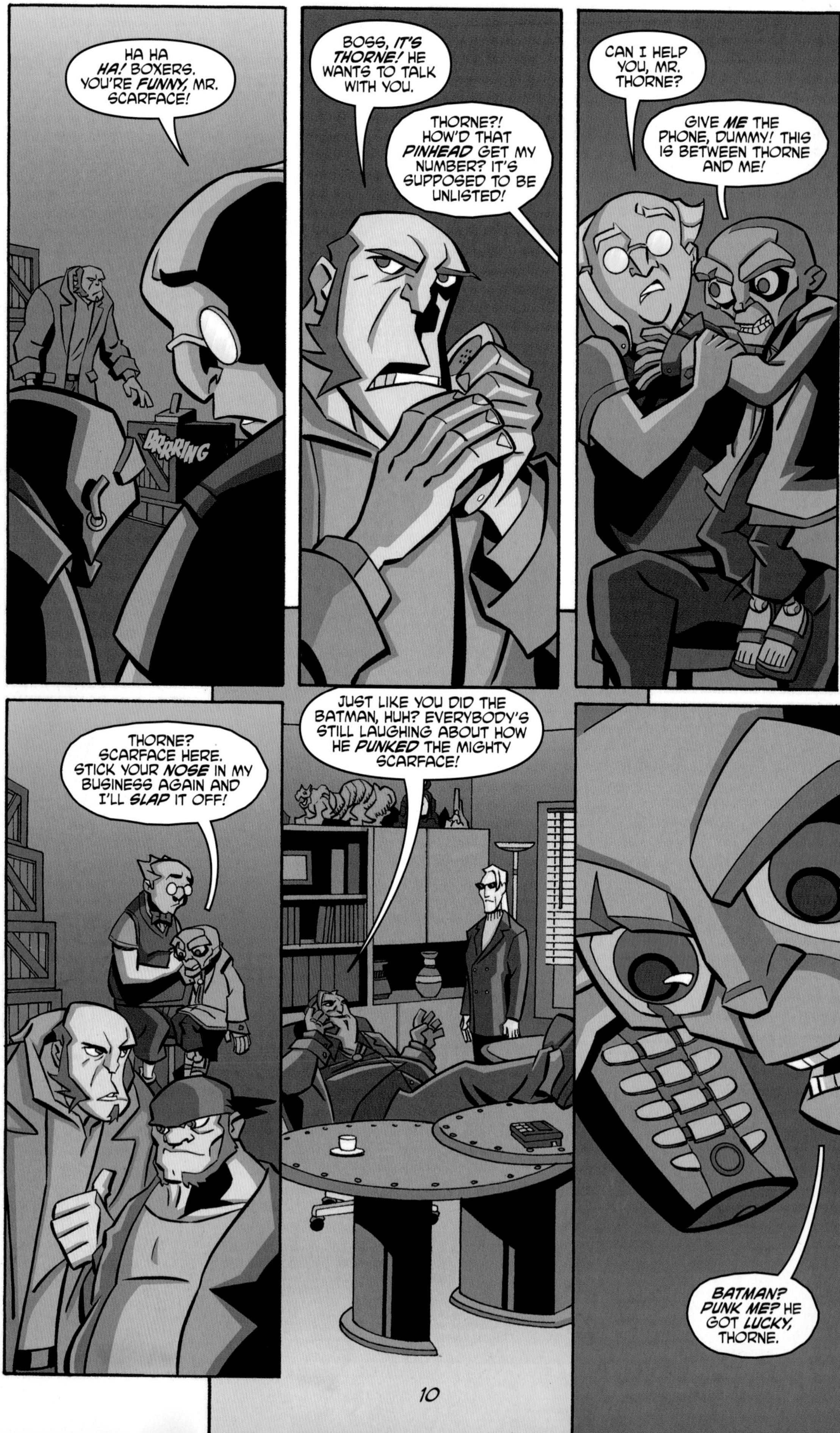
HA HA *HA!* BOXERS. YOU'RE *FUNNY,* MR. SCARFACE!
BRRRING
BOSS, *IT'S THORNE!* HE WANTS TO TALK WITH YOU.
THORNE?! HOW'D THAT *PINHEAD* GET MY NUMBER? IT'S SUPPOSED TO BE UNLISTED!
CAN I HELP YOU, MR. THORNE?
GIVE *ME* THE PHONE, DUMMY! THIS IS BETWEEN THORNE AND ME!
THORNE? SCARFACE HERE. STICK YOUR *NOSE* IN MY BUSINESS AGAIN AND I'LL *SLAP* IT OFF!
JUST LIKE YOU DID THE BATMAN, HUH? EVERYBODY'S STILL LAUGHING ABOUT HOW HE *PUNKED* THE MIGHTY SCARFACE!
BATMAN? PUNK ME? HE GOT *LUCKY,* THORNE.

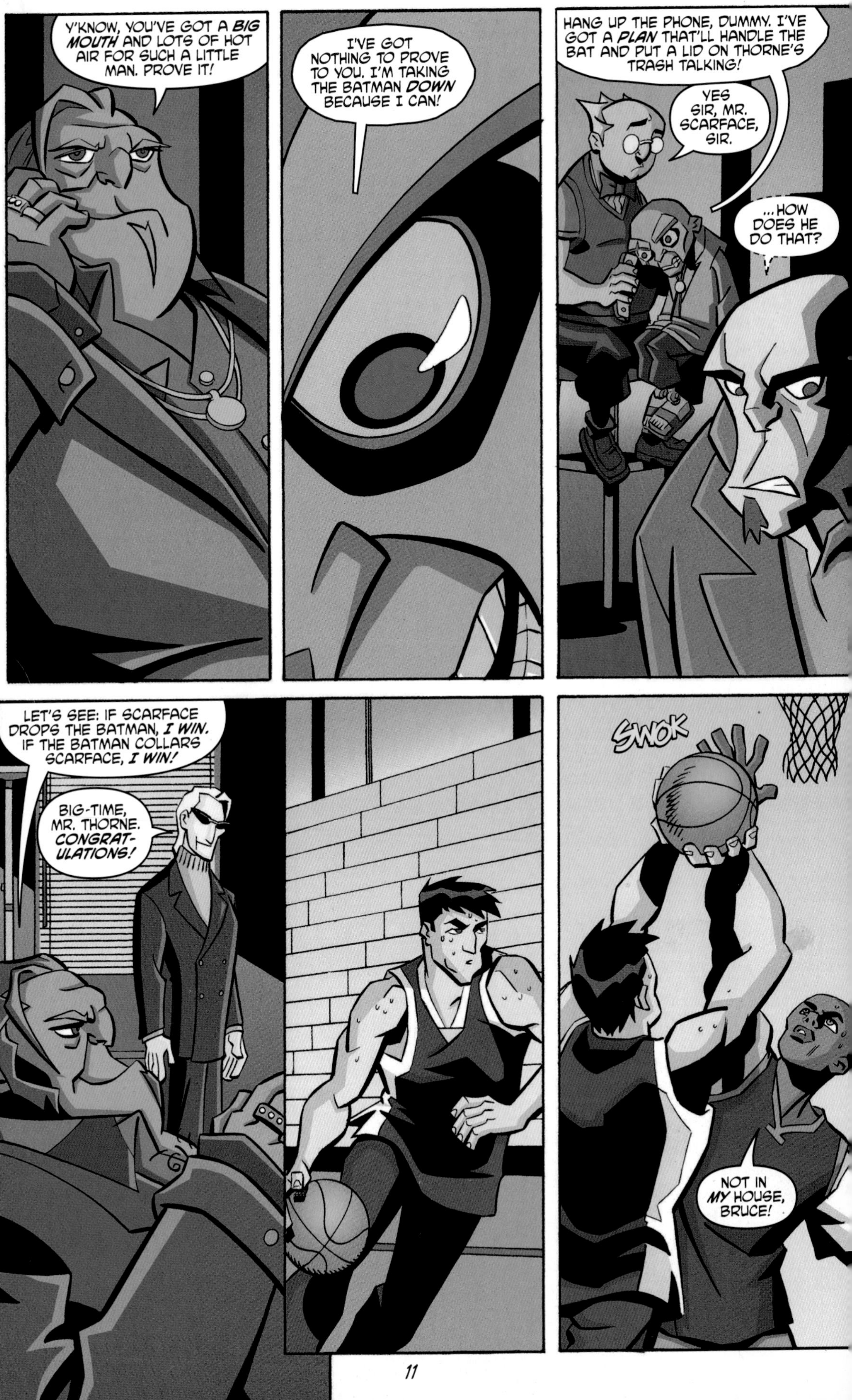
Y'KNOW, YOU'VE GOT A BIG MOUTH AND LOTS OF HOT AIR FOR SUCH A LITTLE MAN. PROVE IT!
I'VE GOT NOTHING TO PROVE TO YOU. I'M TAKING THE BATMAN DOWN BECAUSE I CAN!
HANG UP THE PHONE, DUMMY. I'VE GOT A PLAN THAT'LL HANDLE THE BAT AND PUT A LID ON THORNE'S TRASH TALKING!
YES SIR, MR. SCARFACE, SIR.
...HOW DOES HE DO THAT?
LET'S SEE: IF SCARFACE DROPS THE BATMAN, I WIN. IF THE BATMAN COLLARS SCARFACE, I WIN!
BIG-TIME, MR. THORNE. CONGRAT-ULATIONS!
SWOK
NOT IN MY HOUSE, BRUCE!

NICE MOVE, *ETHAN*. YOU'VE STILL GOT PLENTY OF HOPS.

I WISH. PLUS, IT'S NOT *MY* HOUSE. I'M JUST HERE FOR THE HOOPS AND THE HOT WINGS.

SOMETIMES I FEEL LIKE YOU'VE SPENT TWENTY YEARS KICKING MY BUTT ON THE COURT.

ALMOST. WE MET A FEW MONTHS AFTER *YOUR* PARENTS...

HEY, I'M SORRY ABOUT THAT, MAN. I KNOW IT TOOK YOU A LOT OF YEARS TO RECOVER FROM WHAT HAPPENED.

I NEVER DID. AND DON'T SWEAT IT.

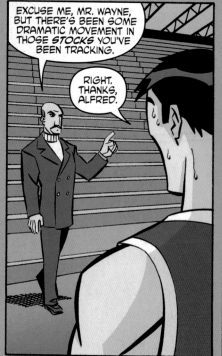

EXCUSE ME, MR. WAYNE, BUT THERE'S BEEN SOME DRAMATIC MOVEMENT IN THOSE *STOCKS* YOU'VE BEEN TRACKING.

RIGHT. THANKS, ALFRED.

TRACKING STOCKS? IT'S 6:00 AT NIGHT.

THREE WORDS: AFTER-HOURS MARKET.

LOOKS LIKE I'M ABOUT TO GET BUSY, TOO. DUTY AND MY DEDICATED PARTNER CALLS. LATER, BRUCE.

BE SAFE, ETHAN.

BEEP BEEP

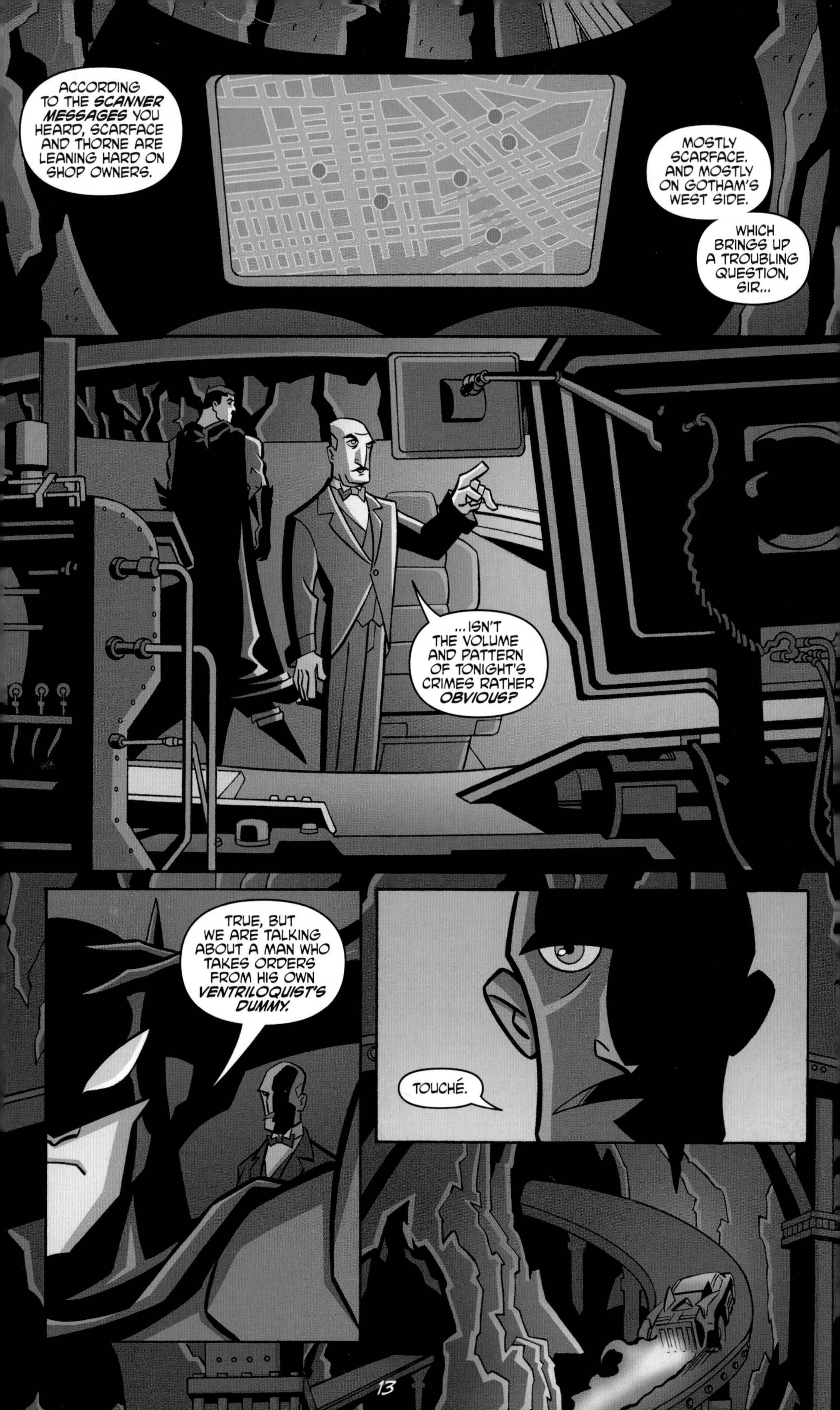
ACCORDING TO THE SCANNER MESSAGES YOU HEARD, SCARFACE AND THORNE ARE LEANING HARD ON SHOP OWNERS.
MOSTLY SCARFACE. AND MOSTLY ON GOTHAM'S WEST SIDE.
WHICH BRINGS UP A TROUBLING QUESTION, SIR...
...ISN'T THE VOLUME AND PATTERN OF TONIGHT'S CRIMES RATHER OBVIOUS?
TRUE, BUT WE ARE TALKING ABOUT A MAN WHO TAKES ORDERS FROM HIS OWN VENTRILOQUIST'S DUMMY.
TOUCHÉ.

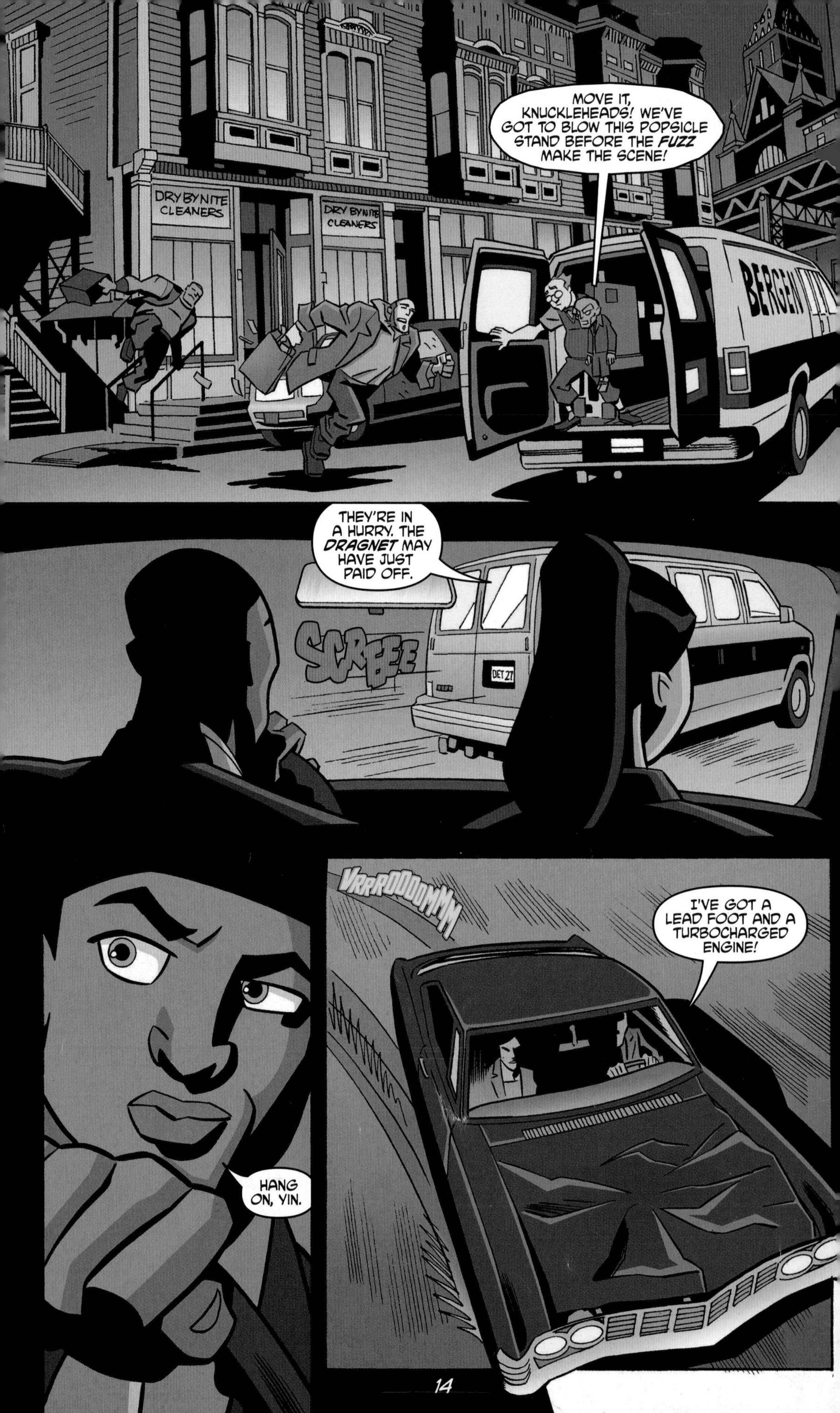
DRY BY NITE CLEANERS
DRY BY NITE CLEANERS
MOVE IT, KNUCKLEHEADS! WE'VE GOT TO BLOW THIS POPSICLE STAND BEFORE THE *FUZZ* MAKE THE SCENE!
BERGEN
THEY'RE IN A HURRY. THE *DRAGNET* MAY HAVE JUST PAID OFF.
SCREEE
DET 27
HANG ON, YIN.
VRRROOOOMMM
I'VE GOT A LEAD FOOT AND A TURBOCHARGED ENGINE!

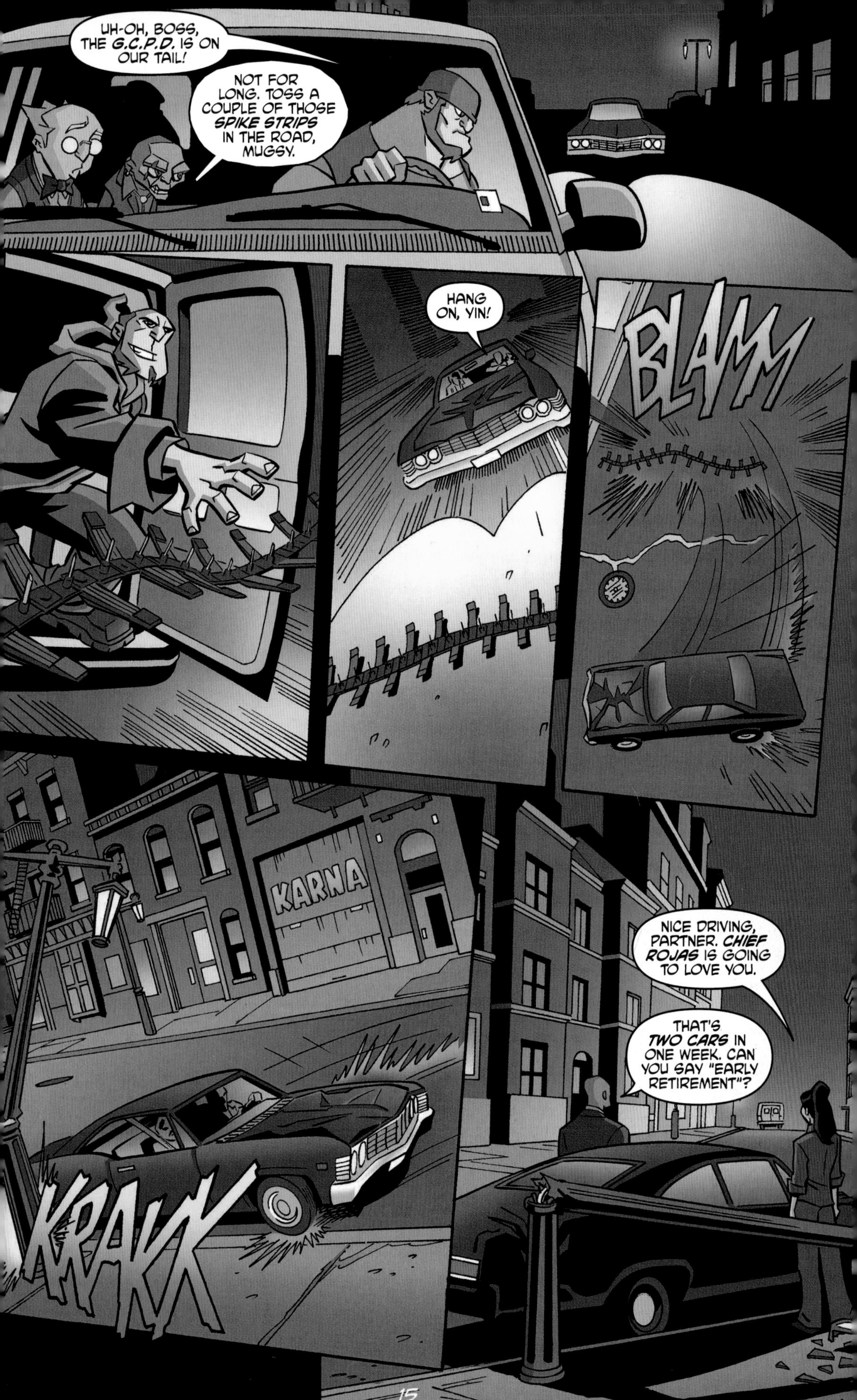
UH-OH, BOSS, THE G.C.P.D. IS ON OUR TAIL!
NOT FOR LONG. TOSS A COUPLE OF THOSE SPIKE STRIPS IN THE ROAD, MUGSY.
HANG ON, YIN!
BLAMM
KARNA
KRAKK
NICE DRIVING, PARTNER. CHIEF ROJAS IS GOING TO LOVE YOU.
THAT'S TWO CARS IN ONE WEEK. CAN YOU SAY "EARLY RETIREMENT"?

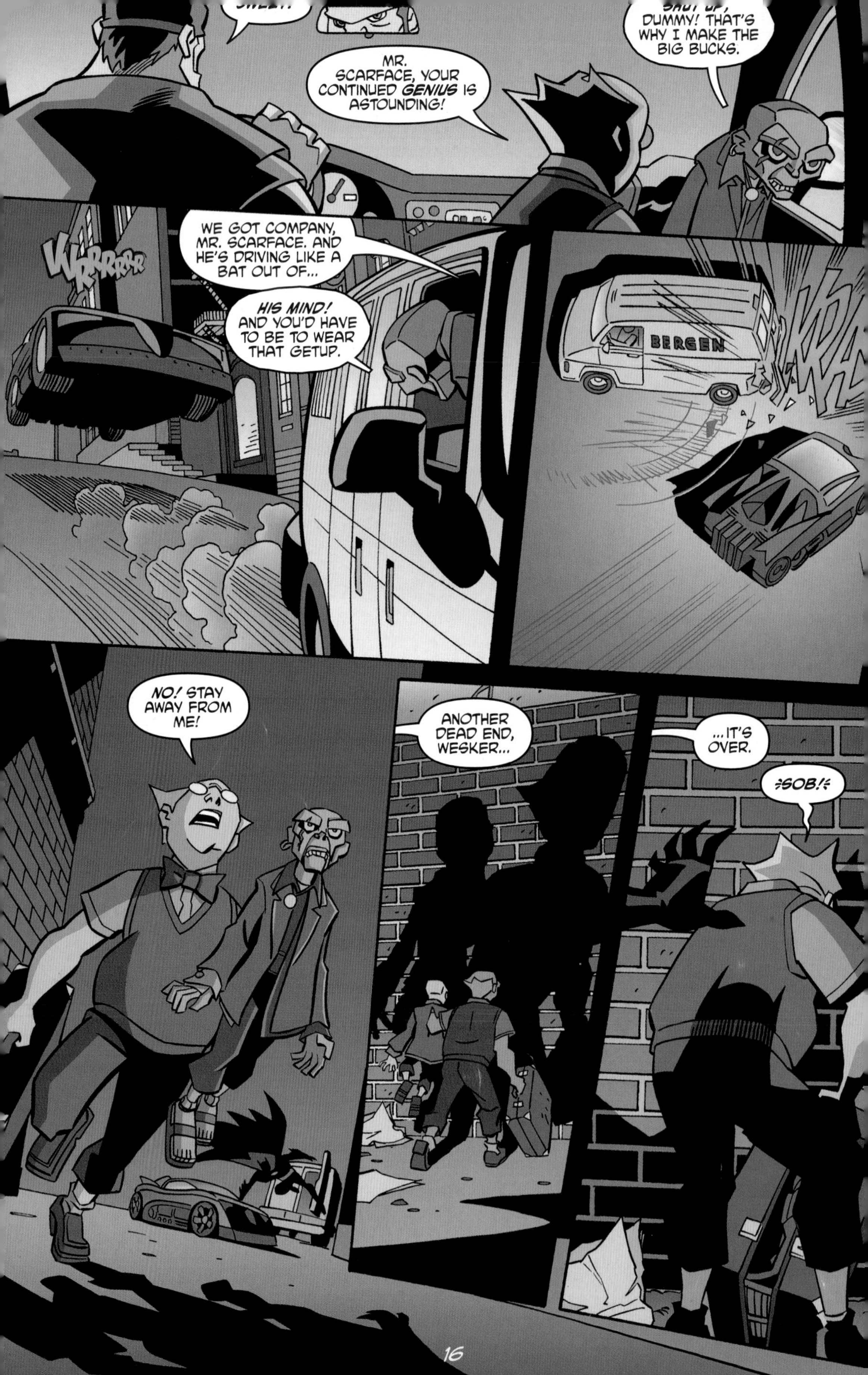
MR. SCARFACE, YOUR CONTINUED GENIUS IS ASTOUNDING!
DUMMY! THAT'S WHY I MAKE THE BIG BUCKS.
VVRRRRRR
WE GOT COMPANY, MR. SCARFACE. AND HE'S DRIVING LIKE A BAT OUT OF...
HIS MIND! AND YOU'D HAVE TO BE TO WEAR THAT GETUP.
BERGEN
KRAK
NO! STAY AWAY FROM ME!
ANOTHER DEAD END, WESKER...
...IT'S OVER.
SOB!

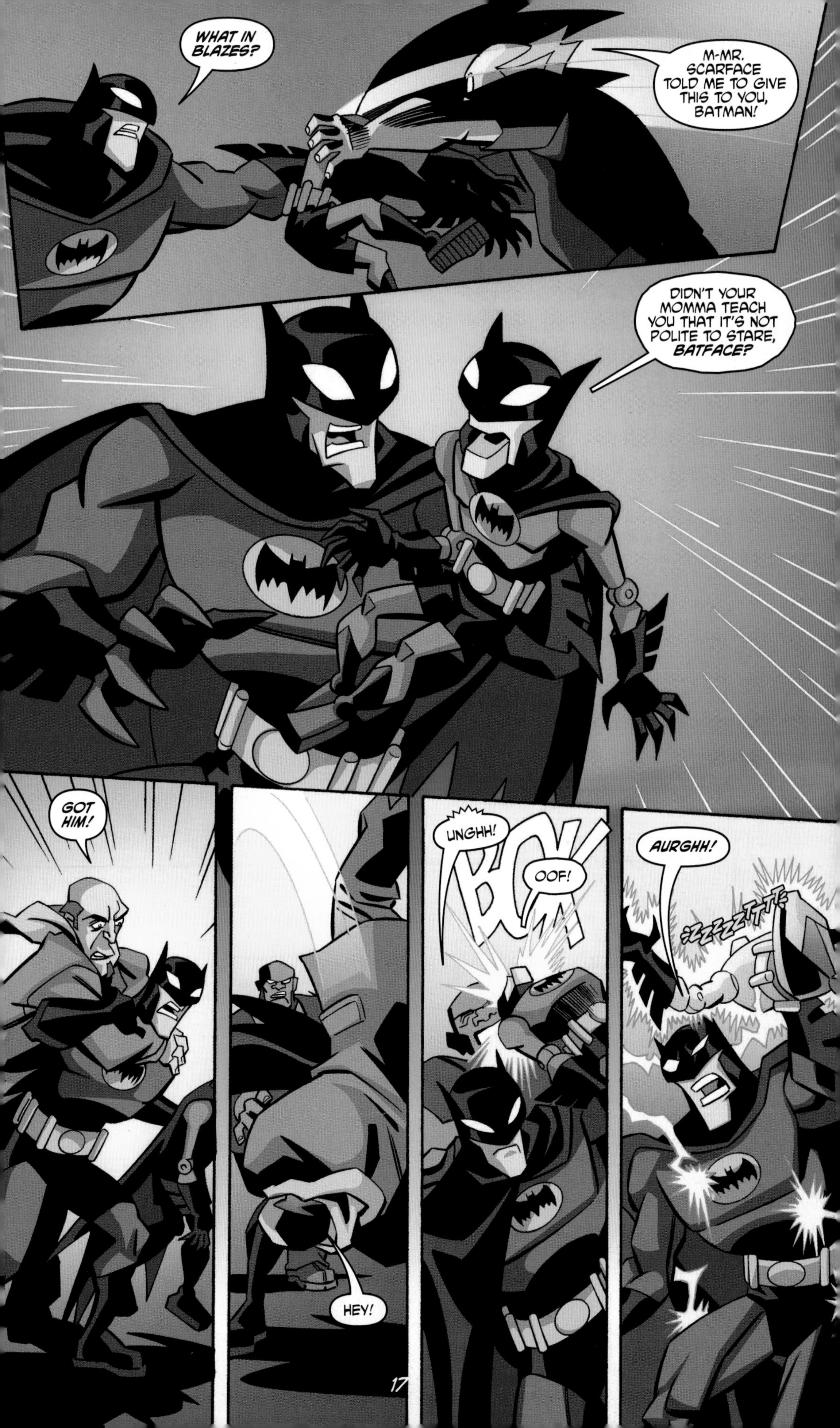
WHAT IN BLAZES?
M-MR. SCARFACE TOLD ME TO GIVE THIS TO YOU, BATMAN!
DIDN'T YOUR MOMMA TEACH YOU THAT IT'S NOT POLITE TO STARE, BATFACE?
GOT HIM!
HEY!
UNGHH!
BOK!
OOF!
AURGHH!
ZZZZZTTT

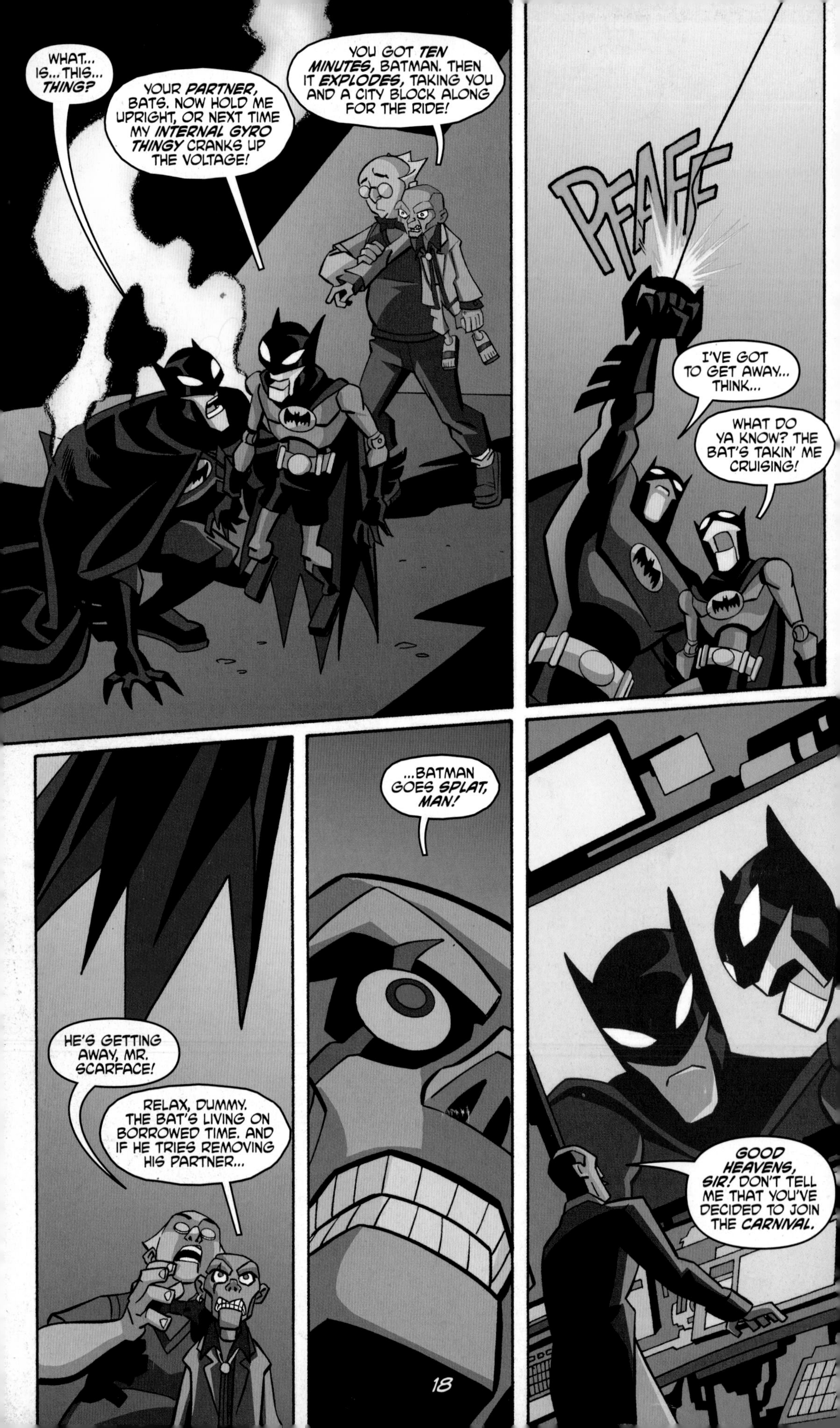
WHAT... IS... THIS... THING?
YOUR PARTNER, BATS. NOW HOLD ME UPRIGHT, OR NEXT TIME MY INTERNAL GYRO THINGY CRANKS UP THE VOLTAGE!
YOU GOT TEN MINUTES, BATMAN. THEN IT EXPLODES, TAKING YOU AND A CITY BLOCK ALONG FOR THE RIDE!
PFAFFF
I'VE GOT TO GET AWAY... THINK...
WHAT DO YA KNOW? THE BAT'S TAKIN' ME CRUISING!
HE'S GETTING AWAY, MR. SCARFACE!
RELAX, DUMMY. THE BAT'S LIVING ON BORROWED TIME. AND IF HE TRIES REMOVING HIS PARTNER...
...BATMAN GOES SPLAT, MAN!
GOOD HEAVENS, SIR! DON'T TELL ME THAT YOU'VE DECIDED TO JOIN THE CARNIVAL.

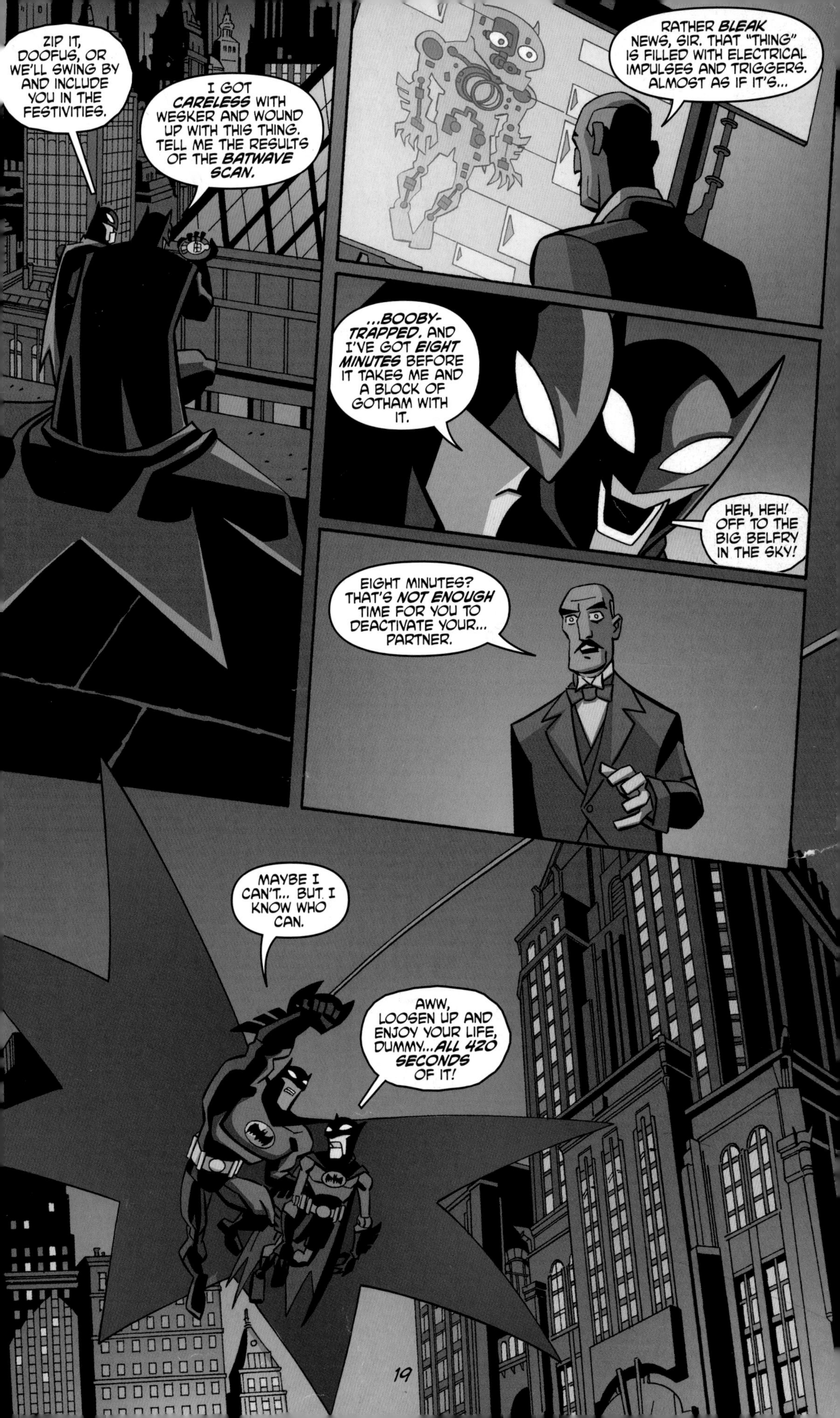
ZIP IT, DOOFUS, OR WE'LL SWING BY AND INCLUDE YOU IN THE FESTIVITIES.
I GOT CARELESS WITH WESKER AND WOUND UP WITH THIS THING. TELL ME THE RESULTS OF THE BATWAVE SCAN.
RATHER BLEAK NEWS, SIR. THAT "THING" IS FILLED WITH ELECTRICAL IMPULSES AND TRIGGERS. ALMOST AS IF IT'S...
...BOOBY-TRAPPED. AND I'VE GOT EIGHT MINUTES BEFORE IT TAKES ME AND A BLOCK OF GOTHAM WITH IT.
HEH, HEH! OFF TO THE BIG BELFRY IN THE SKY!
EIGHT MINUTES? THAT'S NOT ENOUGH TIME FOR YOU TO DEACTIVATE YOUR... PARTNER.
MAYBE I CAN'T... BUT I KNOW WHO CAN.
AWW, LOOSEN UP AND ENJOY YOUR LIFE, DUMMY...ALL 420 SECONDS OF IT!

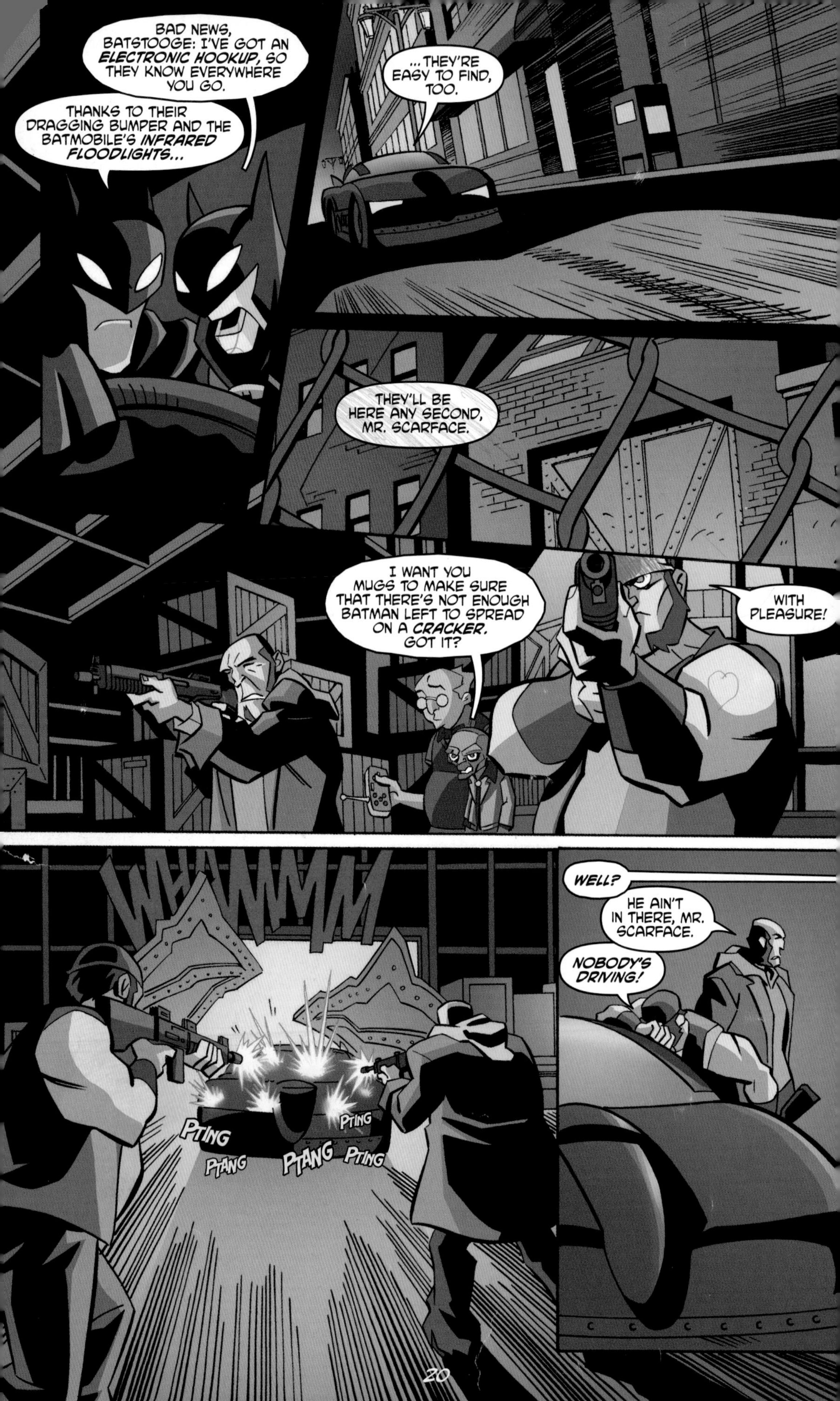
BAD NEWS, BATSTOOGE: I'VE GOT AN ELECTRONIC HOOKUP, SO THEY KNOW EVERYWHERE YOU GO.
THANKS TO THEIR DRAGGING BUMPER AND THE BATMOBILE'S INFRARED FLOODLIGHTS...
...THEY'RE EASY TO FIND, TOO.
THEY'LL BE HERE ANY SECOND, MR. SCARFACE.
I WANT YOU MUGS TO MAKE SURE THAT THERE'S NOT ENOUGH BATMAN LEFT TO SPREAD ON A CRACKER. GOT IT?
WITH PLEASURE!
WHAMMM
PTING
PTANG
PTANG
PTING
PTING
WELL?
HE AIN'T IN THERE, MR. SCARFACE.
NOBODY'S DRIVING!

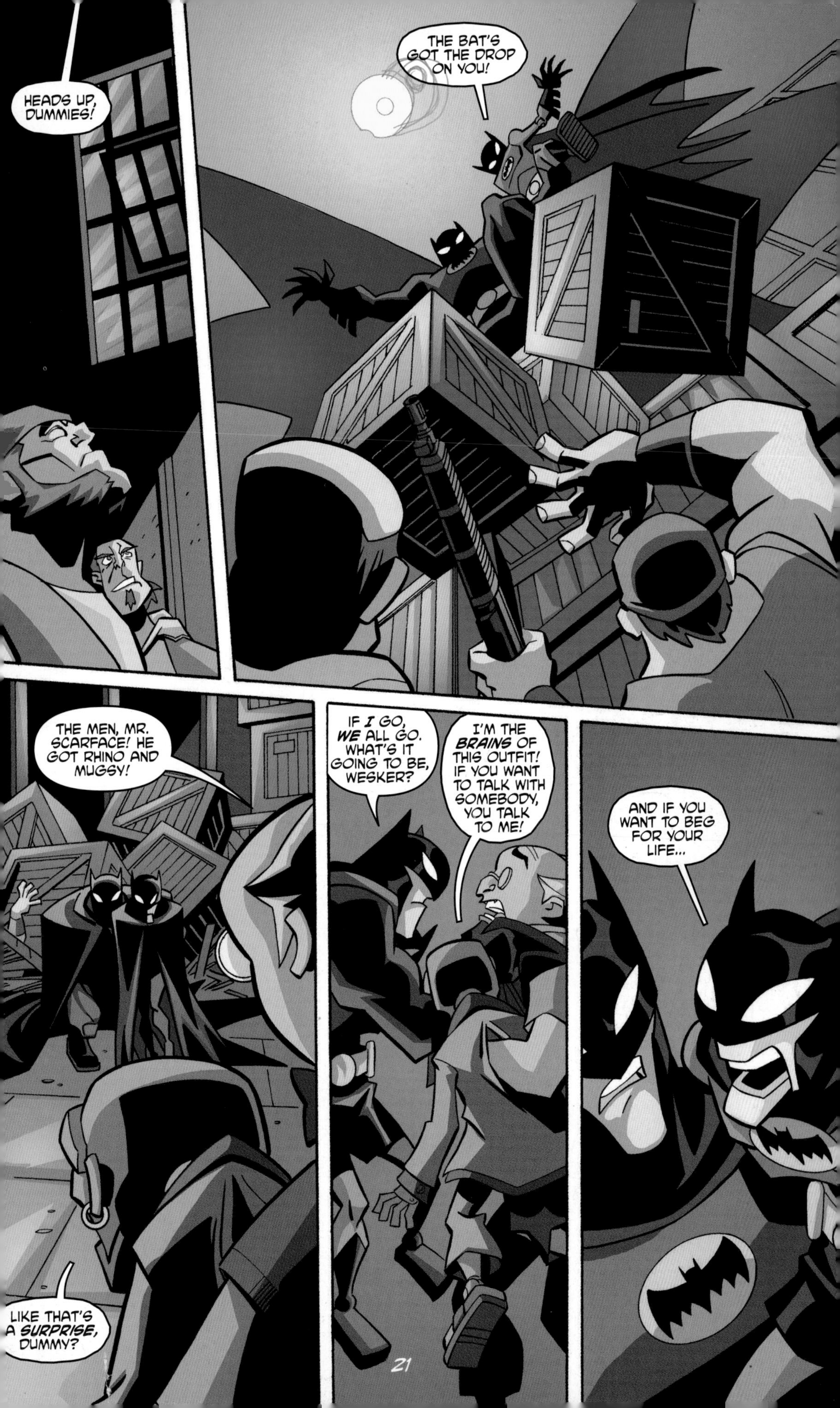
HEADS UP, DUMMIES!
THE BAT'S GOT THE DROP ON YOU!
THE MEN, MR. SCARFACE! HE GOT RHINO AND MUGSY!
LIKE THAT'S A *SURPRISE*, DUMMY?
IF *I* GO, *WE* ALL GO. WHAT'S IT GOING TO BE, WESKER?
I'M THE *BRAINS* OF THIS OUTFIT! IF YOU WANT TO TALK WITH SOMEBODY, YOU TALK TO ME!
AND IF YOU WANT TO BEG FOR YOUR LIFE...

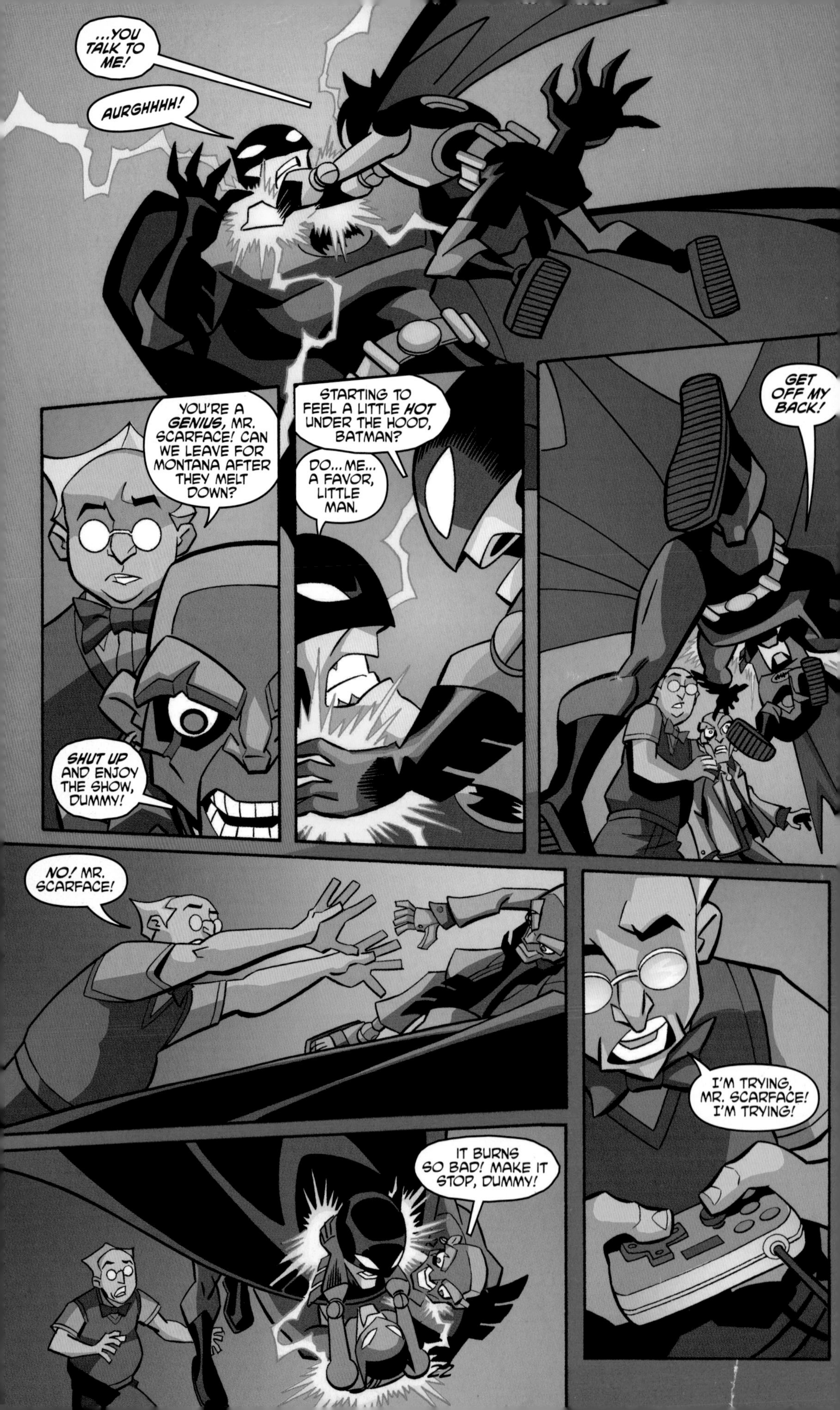

...YOU TALK TO ME!
AURGHHHH!
YOU'RE A *GENIUS*, MR. SCARFACE! CAN WE LEAVE FOR MONTANA AFTER THEY MELT DOWN?
SHUT UP AND ENJOY THE SHOW, DUMMY!
STARTING TO FEEL A LITTLE *HOT* UNDER THE HOOD, BATMAN?
DO...ME... A FAVOR, LITTLE MAN.
GET OFF MY BACK!
NO! MR. SCARFACE!
I'M TRYING, MR. SCARFACE! I'M TRYING!
IT BURNS SO BAD! MAKE IT STOP, DUMMY!

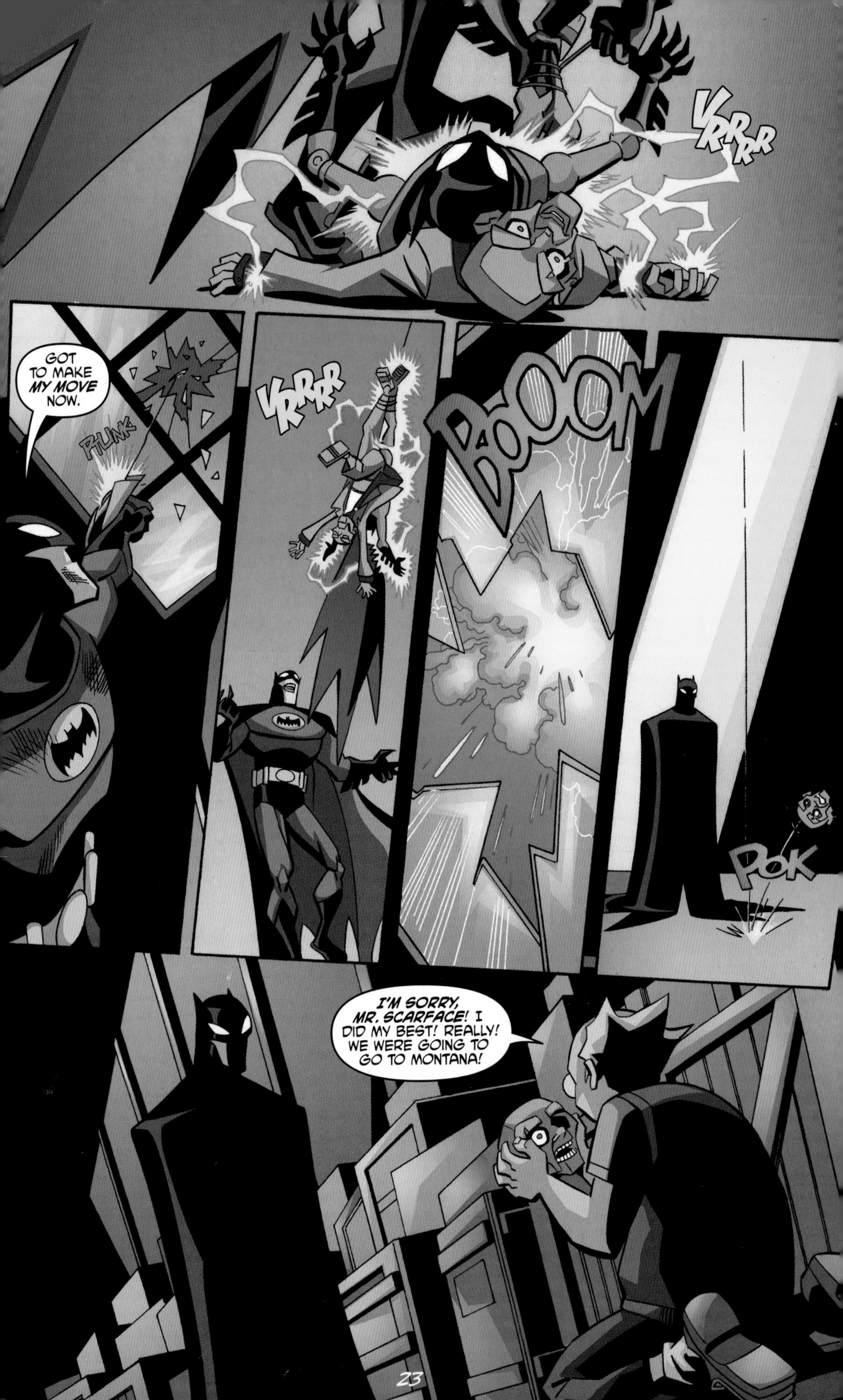
VRRRR
GOT TO MAKE *MY MOVE* NOW.
PTUNK
VRRRR
BOOOM
POK
I'M SORRY, MR. SCARFACE! I DID MY BEST! REALLY! WE WERE GOING TO GO TO MONTANA!

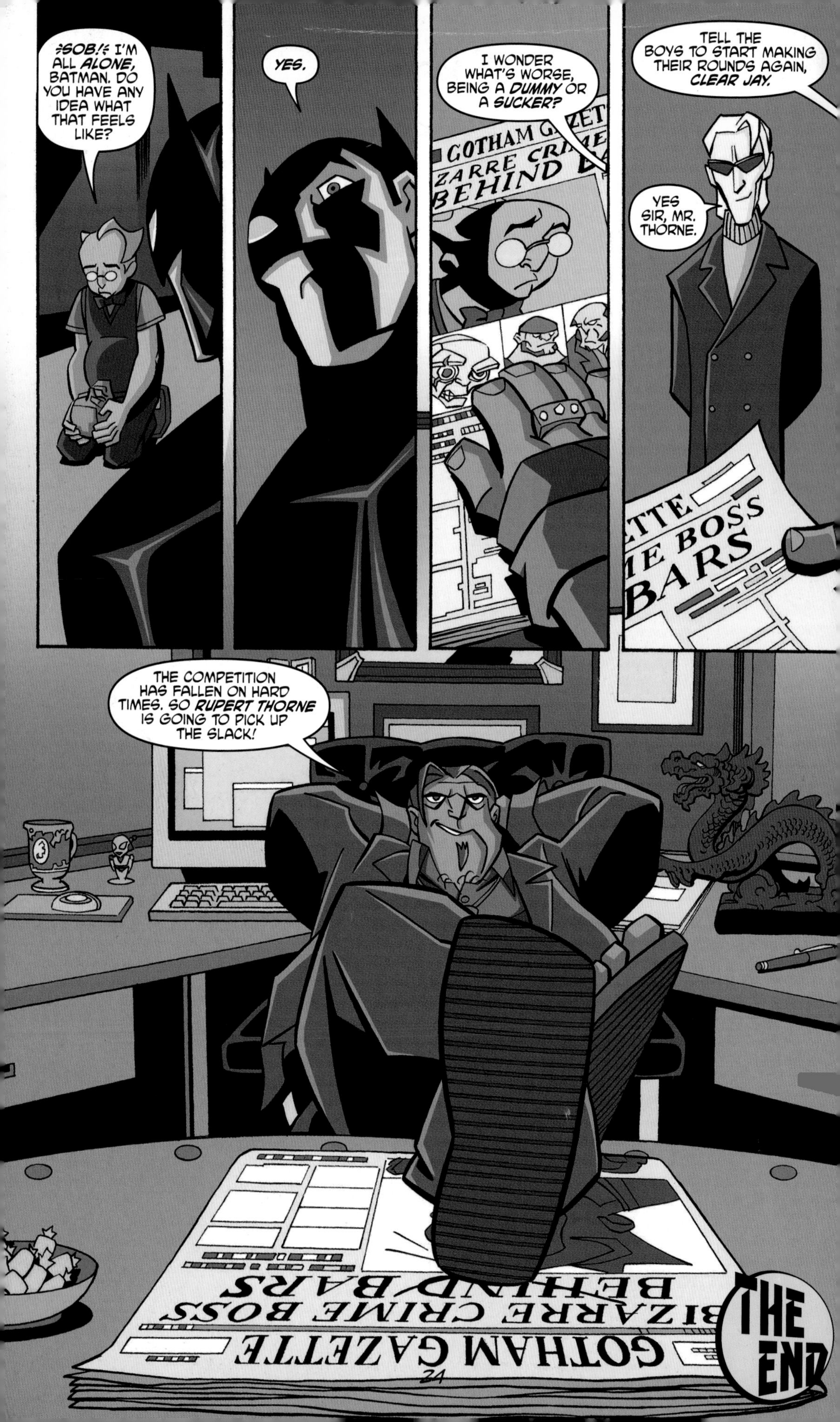

SOB! I'M ALL ALONE, BATMAN. DO YOU HAVE ANY IDEA WHAT THAT FEELS LIKE?
YES.
I WONDER WHAT'S WORSE, BEING A DUMMY OR A SUCKER?
GOTHAM GAZETTE
BIZARRE CRIME BOSS BEHIND BARS
TELL THE BOYS TO START MAKING THEIR ROUNDS AGAIN, CLEAR JAY.
YES SIR, MR. THORNE.
THE COMPETITION HAS FALLEN ON HARD TIMES. SO RUPERT THORNE IS GOING TO PICK UP THE SLACK!
GOTHAM GAZETTE
BIZARRE CRIME BOSS BEHIND BARS
THE END

CREATORS

BILL MATHENY WRITER

Along with comics like THE BATMAN STRIKES, Bill Matheny has written for TV series including KRYPTO THE SUPERDOG, WHERE'S WALDO, A PUP NAMED SCOOBY-DOO, and many others.

CHRISTOPHER JONES PENCILLER

Christopher Jones is an artist that has worked for DC Comics, Image, Malibu, Caliber, and Sundragon Comics.

TERRY BEATTY INKER

Terry Beatty has inked THE BATMAN STRIKES! and BATMAN: THE BRAVE AND THE BOLD as well as several other DC Comics graphic novels.

GLOSSARY

astounding (uh-STOUN-ding)--causing a feeling of great surprise or wonder

belfry (BELL-free)--a tower where a bell hangs. Bats are often seen in belfries.

bleak (BLEEK)--not warm, friendly, cheerful, or hopeful

carnival (KAR-ni-vuhl)--a form of entertainment that travels to different places that has rides and games

dedicated (ded-uh-KAY-tid)--having very strong support for or loyalty to a person, group, or cause

dramatic (druh-MAT-ik)--sudden and extreme

dummy (DUM-ee)--a doll that is shaped like a person that is used as a puppet

racket (RAK-et)--a criminal scheme or activity intended to trick people out of their money

slack (SLAK)--lacking the expected or desired activity

vigilante (vij-uh-LAN-tee)--a person who is not a police officer but who tries to catch and punish criminals

VISUAL QUESTIONS & PROMPTS

1. Why do you think half of Batman's face is visible here? Why does Batman say he knows how Wesker feels?

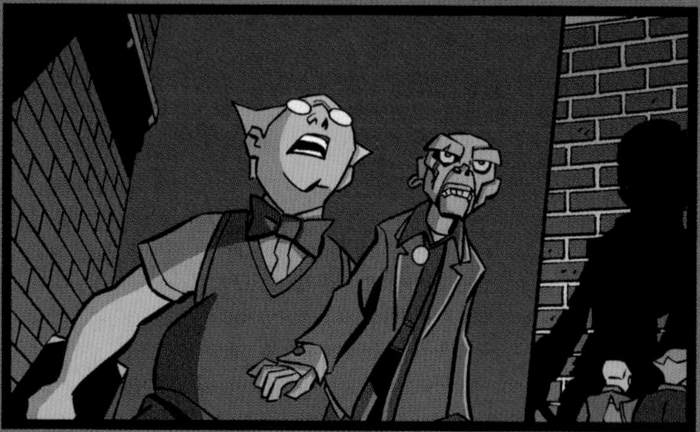

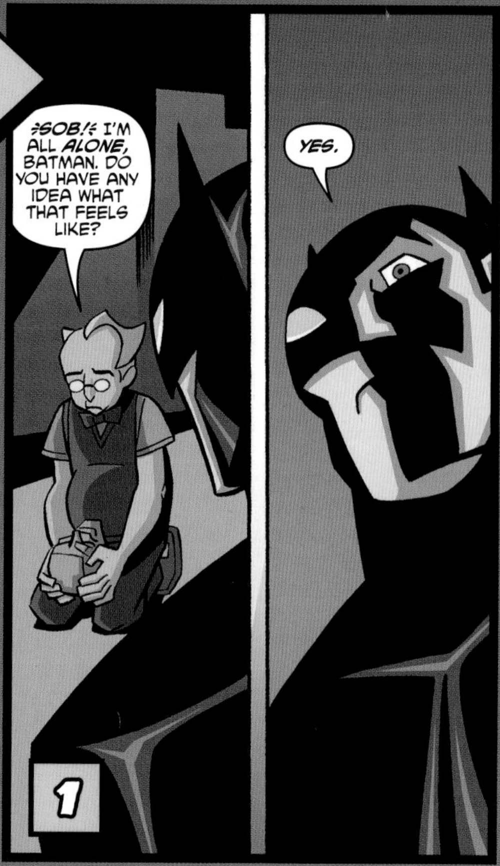

SOB! I'M ALL *ALONE,* BATMAN. DO YOU HAVE ANY IDEA WHAT THAT FEELS LIKE?
YES.
1

2. In this panel, the red sound effect is overlapped by part of the art [the door]. The yellow sound effects, on the other hand, overlap the art. Why do you think this is the case?

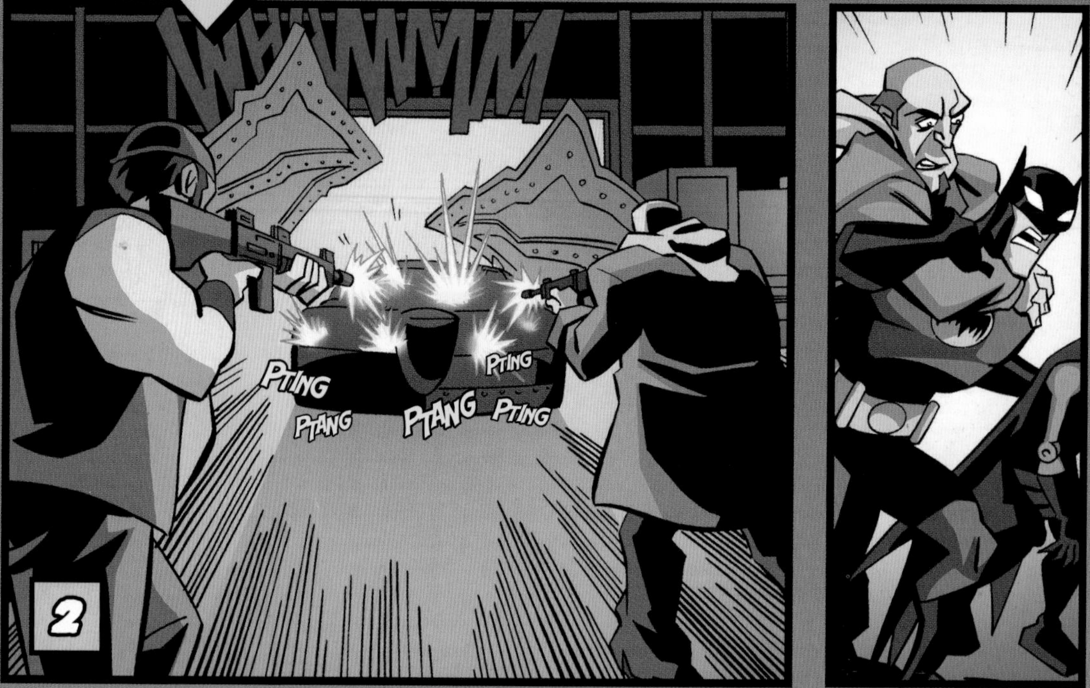

WHAMMM
PTING
PTANG
PTANG
PTING
PTING
2

3. Why do you think Scarface chose to create an explosive puppet in his attempt to defeat Batman?

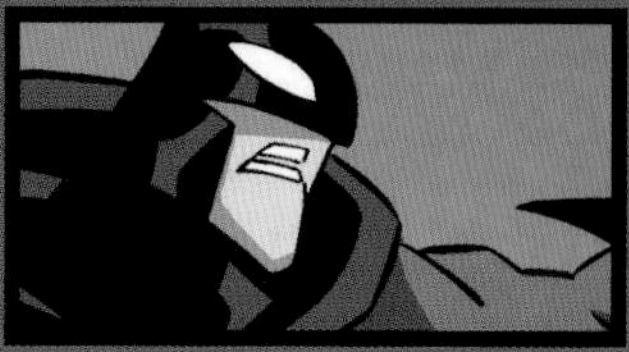

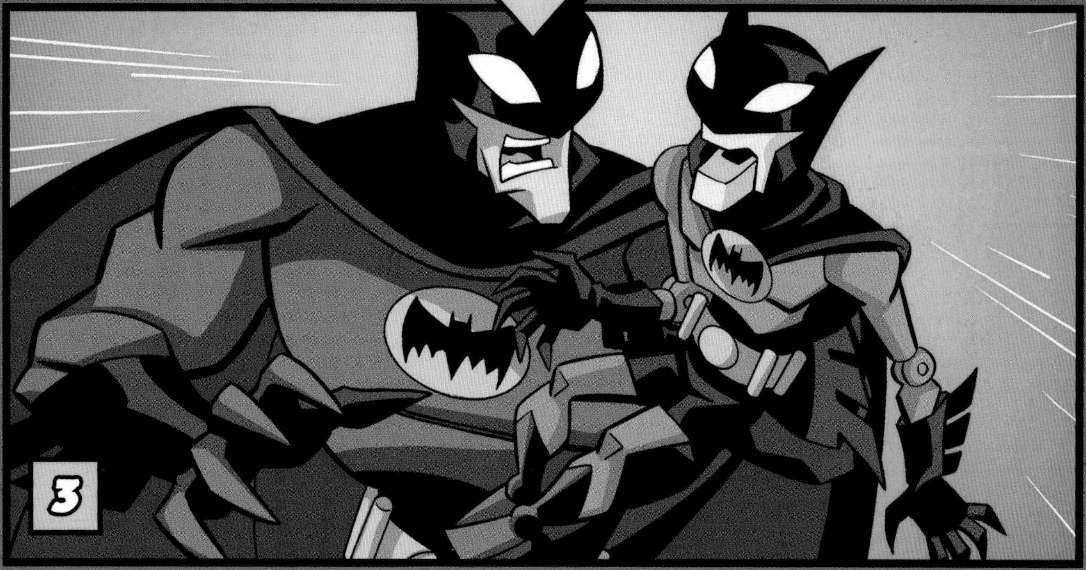
3

4. Scarface has a scar over one eye. Write a short story about how the puppet got its scar.

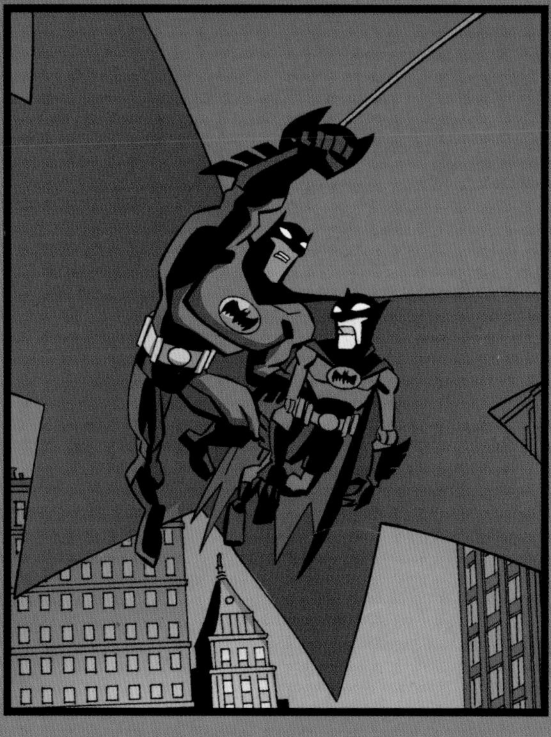

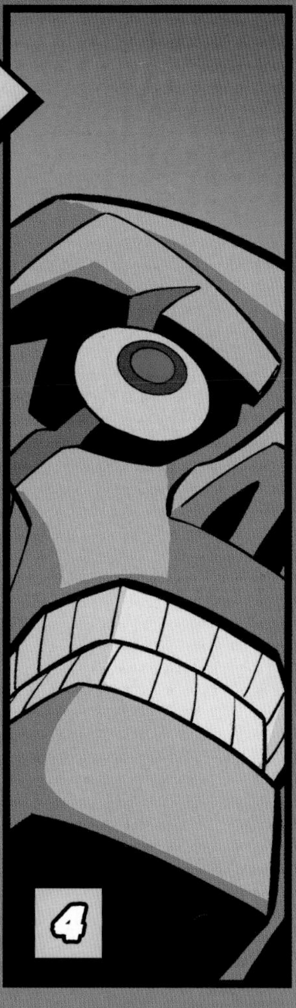
4

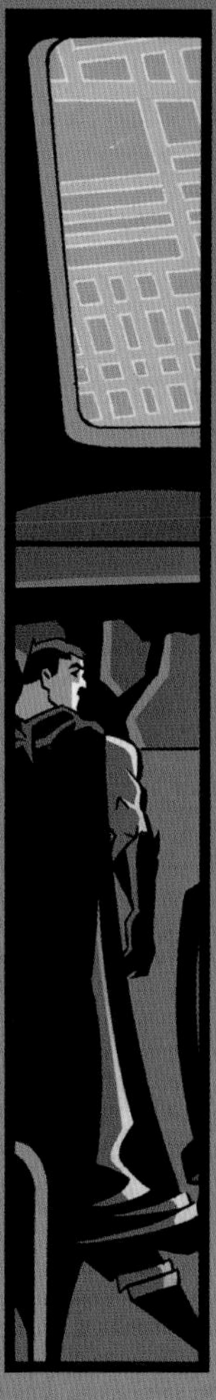

READ THEM ALL!

THE BATMAN STRIKES!

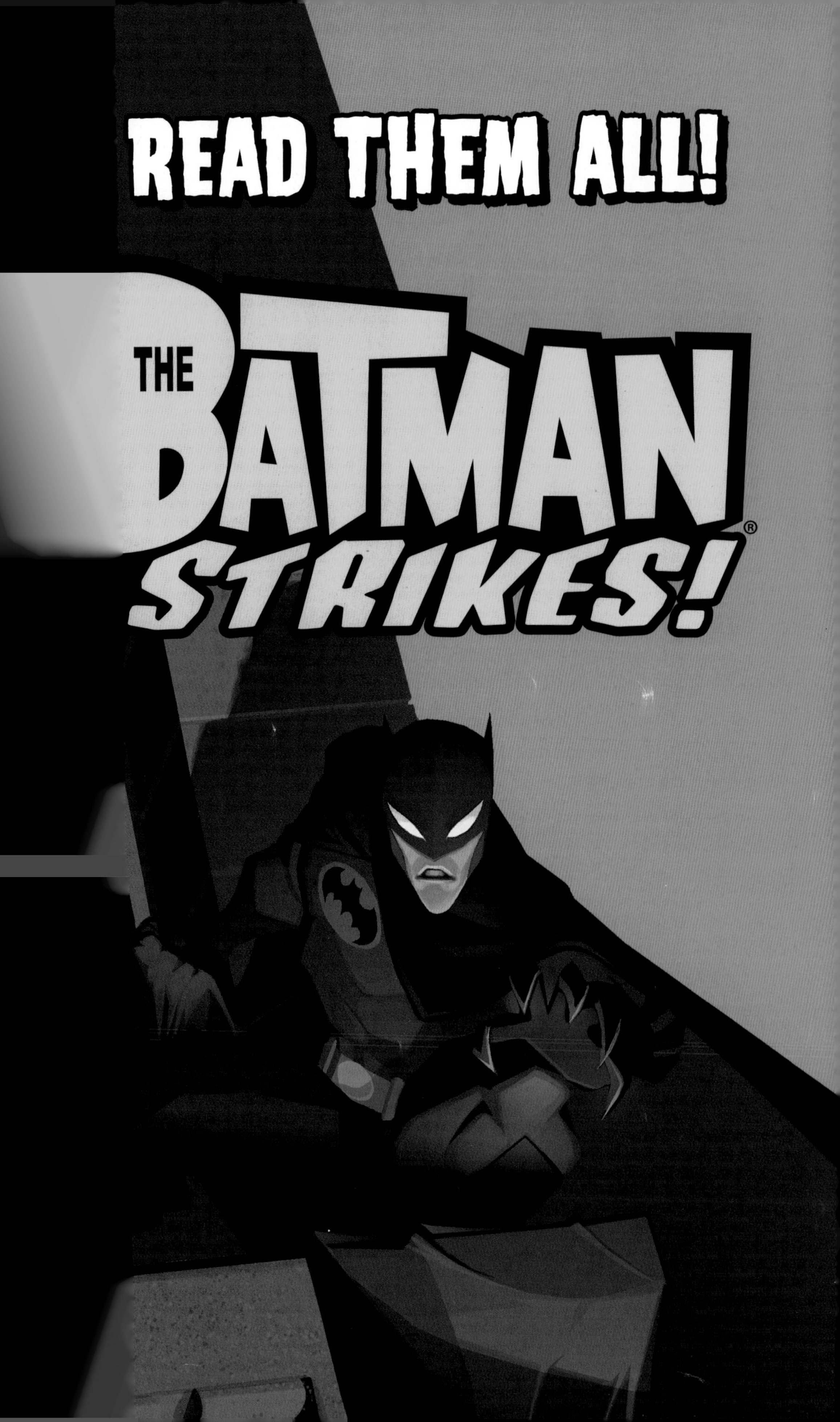

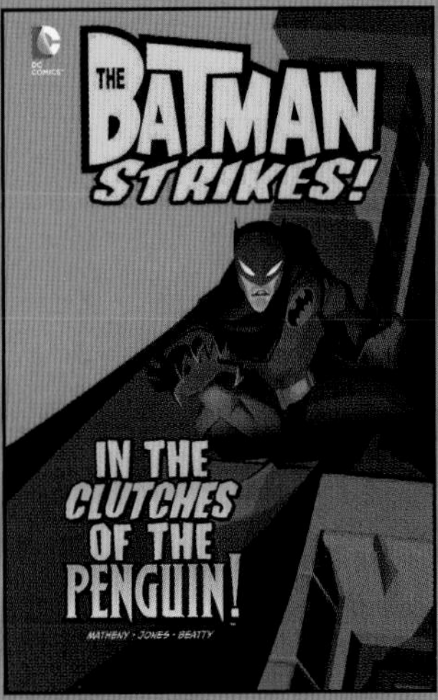
DC COMICS
THE BATMAN STRIKES!
IN THE CLUTCHES OF THE PENGUIN!
MATHENY · JONES · BEATTY

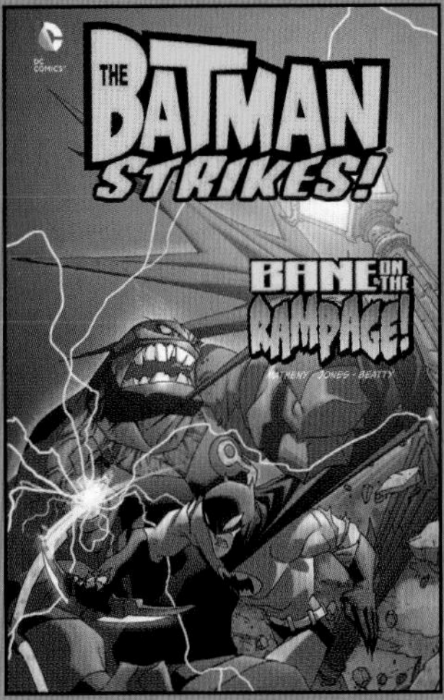
DC COMICS
THE BATMAN STRIKES!
BANE ON THE RAMPAGE!
MATHENY · JONES · BEATTY

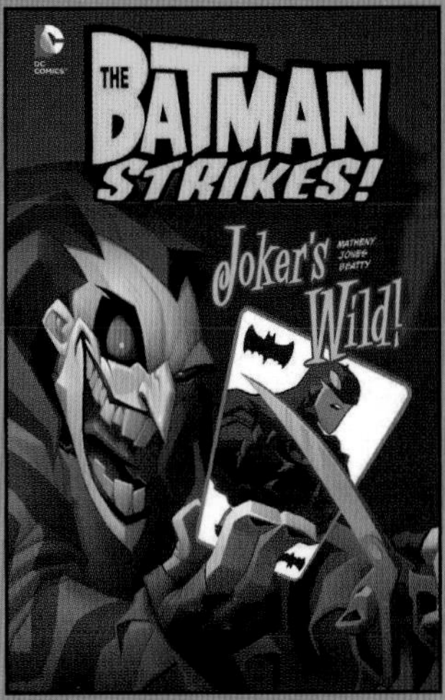
DC COMICS
THE BATMAN STRIKES!
Joker's Wild!
MATHENY JONES BEATTY

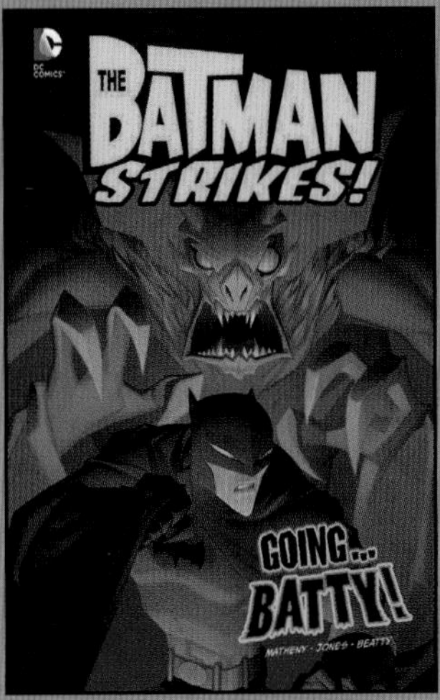
DC COMICS
THE BATMAN STRIKES!
GOING... BATTY!
MATHENY · JONES · BEATTY

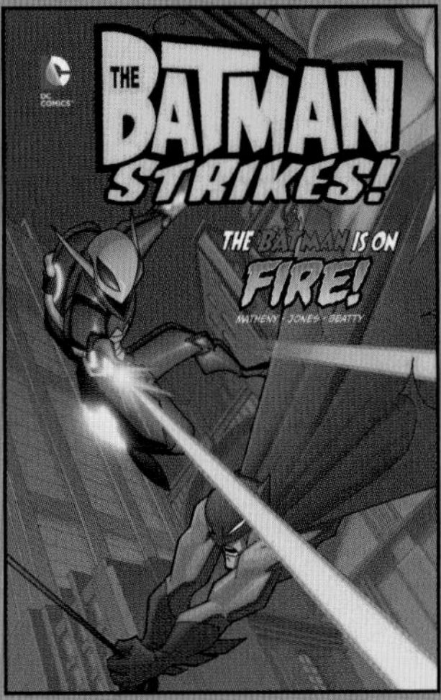
DC COMICS
THE BATMAN STRIKES!
THE BATMAN IS ON FIRE!
MATHENY · JONES · BEATTY

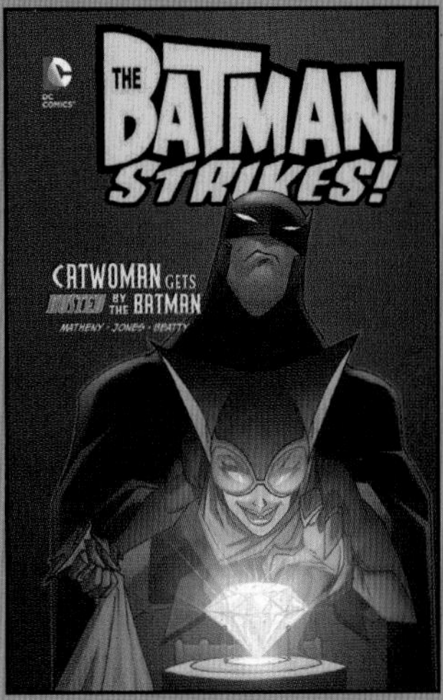
DC COMICS
THE BATMAN STRIKES!
CATWOMAN GETS BUSTED BY THE BATMAN
MATHENY · JONES · BEATTY

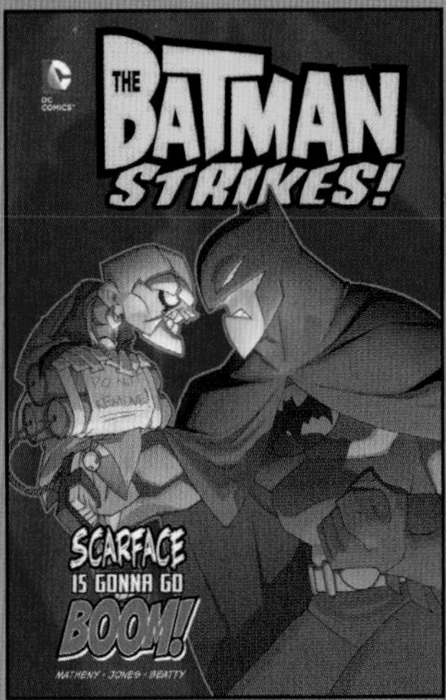
DC COMICS
THE BATMAN STRIKES!
SCARFACE IS GONNA GO BOOM!
MATHENY · JONES · BEATTY

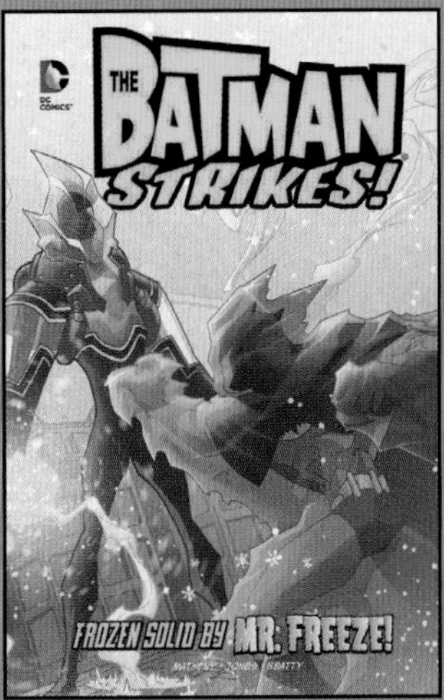
DC COMICS
THE BATMAN STRIKES!
FROZEN SOLID BY MR. FREEZE!
MATHENY · JONES · BEATTY

only from...

STONE ARCH BOOKS™
a capstone imprint www.capstonepub.com

THE BATMAN STRIKES!®

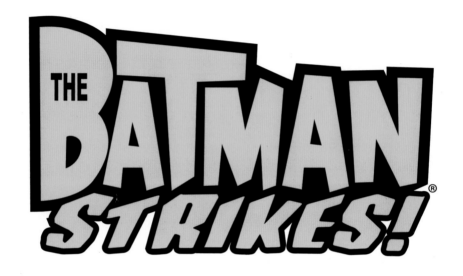